Ghosts in the Gallery

ATHENEUM BOOKS BY BARBARA BROOKS WALLACE

PEPPERMINTS IN THE PARLOR

THE BARREL IN THE BASEMENT

PERFECT ACRES, INC.

THE TWIN IN THE TAVERN

COUSINS IN THE CASTLE

SPARROWS IN THE SCULLERY

GHOSTS IN THE GALLERY

BARBARA BROOKS WALLACE

Ghosts in the Gallery

A JEAN KARL BOOK

ATHENEUM BOOKS *for* YOUNG READERS

NEW YORK LONDON TORONTO SYDNEY SINGAPORE

Atheneum Books for Young Readers
An imprint of Simon & Schuster Children's Publishing Division
1230 Avenue of the Americas
New York, New York 10020

Book design by Michael Nelson
The text of this book is set in Bembo.

Printed in the United States of America
2 4 6 8 10 9 7 5 3 1

Library of Congress Cataloging-in-Publication Data
Wallace, Barbara Brooks, 1922-
Ghosts in the gallery/ Barbara Brooks Wallace.
p.   cm.
"A Jean Karl book."
Summary: When eleven-year-old Jenny arrives at her
grandfather's house but is not recognized as one
of the family because of a servant's intrigue,
the young orphan endures a difficult fate.
ISBN 0-689-83175-7
[1. Orphans-Fiction. 2. Grandfathers-Fiction.] I. Title.
PZ7.W1547Gh   2000   [Fic]—dc21   99-29055

FIRST
EDITION

For Victoria Antonia Wallace
With love and a zillion happy memories
Of zero to twelve

Contents

I	Jenny	1
II	Graymark House	6
III	A Dangerous Mistake	12
IV	Cruel! Cruel!	17
V	Dire Warnings	26
VI	A Puzzling Late-Night Conversation	35
VII	Lilly's Lessons in What's What	40
VIII	Ghosts in the Gallery	46
IX	Jingle	56
X	A Forbidden Visit	61
XI	Friendly Overtures	68
XII	A Surprise in the Stable	75
XIII	Secret Messages	84
XIV	A Theft in the Library	89
XV	A Good and Kind Child	95
XVI	A Terrifying Encounter	100
XVII	A Mysterious Journey	106
XVIII	Grim Revelations	112
XIX	A Joyful Welcome	123

Chapter I

Jenny

𝕿he coach lantern cast an eerie glow through the thick fog swirling past the carriage as it lumbered along the dirt road in the fast-fading light of evening. The drumming of the horses' hooves had a curiously muffled sound inside the carriage, where four travelers sat in silence. Two of them, an elderly couple wrapped in heavy woolen blankets, had their eyes closed. Their heads were nodding. The third was a heavyset man with a round, fleshy face. Every time the carriage hit a rut, his face shook like a rich pudding. Staring stonily out the window, he reached every so often inside his mink-collared cape to pull out a massive gold pocket watch. After holding it up to the window to catch the coach lantern light, he would shake his head in annoyance, impatiently jam the watch back in his pocket, and continue staring moodily out the window.

The fourth traveler in the carriage was a young girl, who knew none of the others. To her, they were all strangers. But was that not all she had in her life now, strangers?

Seated across from the dozing elderly couple, the girl, Jenny, stared at the pale face reflected in the window beside her. Was that unearthly reflection really hers, or did it belong to yet another stranger, a different young girl? But Jenny knew that everything she saw was hers, the pink velveteen bonnet, now travel stained, the white ostrich feather adorning it, now sadly drooping. And those were her golden ringlets, now lank and lifeless. What were definitely not hers, however, were the tears rolling down the face looking back at her. They came simply from the rain that had begun to lace through the fog, and was now drizzling down the window.

In truth, Jenny had not shed any tears now for days. No, it had become weeks. The last had been when she stood at the ship's railing, watching the China coastline fade away in the distance. That was where she had spent all but the first few weeks of her eleven years. But it was not the land itself she cried for. Her tears had been for two people that it held—her beloved papa and her dear, sweet mama, now no more.

From that time on, Jenny's life had been in the hands of strangers. And she had quickly learned that tears soon became tiresome, and sympathy could thin in a hurry. The dried-up woman with whom she had had to share her cabin on the ship, having seen Jenny's tears at the railing, told her that she must be "a brave little girl," and made it clear that she expected Jenny to make herself as little noticed as possible.

The ship's captain and the stewards in whose care she had been placed were all kind to her, but were taken up with their own concerns and could give her little time.

When at last the ocean voyage ended, Jenny's travels were still not over, for she had to take yet another journey, this one by train to the eastern shore of America. It was not so long or so fearsome as the one by sea, but again she was with strangers. And again this was true of the carriage in which she was now traveling. Strangers! Always strangers! Why, Jenny asked herself, could her mama not have managed better and tried to find someone who really cared about her to take her on this long journey, and not just have her passed from the hands of one stranger to another?

But Jenny had no sooner asked herself the question than she was struck with horror at having had such a wicked, ungrateful thought about her darling mama. Mama, who had been left frightened and alone—probably far more than Jenny now was—in a strange, foreign country, with almost no means, when her young husband had been suddenly and cruelly carried off by a terrible illness soon after they had arrived there. Mercifully, being a dancer, Mama had found employment at a small dance studio, where foreigners came for dance lessons and to bring their children for dance lessons as well. In the end, she had married the owner, Felix Bekins.

Felix Bekins had loved Jenny, always wearing a smile on his face as he watched her flitting about the studio, a great pink bow perched like a trembling butterfly on her golden ringlets, and on her cherubic, pink-cheeked face a winning smile that enchanted all who saw her.

And, of course, he had adored Jenny's mama, with her own golden curls, rosy cheeks, and radiant smile, and her twinkling, light-as-a-fairy's toes that barely touched the dance studio floor as she whirled across it in her grand, bright, frilly dresses.

He complained constantly that he wished he could do more for his "little charmers," and that they were not so very poor. For although the handsomely dressed American, British, French, and German ladies and gentlemen who patronized the studio were wealthy, very little of that wealth found its way into dance lessons. So while they all, as was the custom of foreigners in China then, had large households of many servants, Felix Bekins could only provide for his family a small apartment run by but two servants, Ling and his wife, Cho Mei.

But Jenny herself did not care a bit that they did not have half a dozen or more servants, for Cho Mei was her amah, the nursemaid who cared as tenderly for Jenny as did her own mama. Nor did it matter to her that earnings from the studio were so meager she could not attend expensive private schools, the only English-speaking schools available. For after carefree days spent at the studio, she was given reading and writing lessons every night by her Papa

Felix. So her life was a full and happy one despite Papa's complaints.

Then another tragedy befell Mama, and Jenny as well, for Felix Bekins had been struck down with a failing heart, so he, too, was taken from them. Mama had struggled valiantly to keep the studio going, but at last, weakened by all she had endured, she had fallen prey to a deadly illness of the lungs. Before long, the rosy cheeks so loved by Felix Bekins became wan and sunken.

At last it had become clear to her that she might have little time left in this world, and some provision must be made for Jenny when that time had run out. So she went to her desk to write a letter, and from the anguished look on her face, it was clearly a letter she had a great deal of difficulty in writing.

At the time the letter was being written, Jenny was not told the real reason it had to be written at all. Mama had continued to say that she was feeling better day by day, and that the letter was only because she thought it high time she wrote to Jenny's grandfather.

"Grandfather? What grandfather?" Jenny had asked. Was this Papa's father? If so, why was he never mentioned? Why had she never even *heard* of him before?

But it turned out that it was not Papa Felix's father who was to receive the letter, but the father of her "real" papa, the one who had died when she was an infant. It had been such a very long time since Mama had spoken of him, Jenny had come to think that the papa she had recently lost was the *real* one. Now, here was this "real" grandfather being written to because Mama thought it was "high time" she did. Why? Why after all this time write to someone of so little importance in their lives that Jenny had never even been told about him?

Then, finally, Mama knew she could no longer put off telling Jenny the true reason for the letter, and how when Mama was no longer there, Jenny must travel to America to live with this "real" grandfather, the only person left in the world to take care of her.

With the meager funds remaining to her, Mama had, it appeared, already arranged for Jenny's passage.

It seemed that, other than that he was very rich, she could tell Jenny almost nothing about this grandfather, for she had met him but once, and had seen his great house built on a cliff overlooking the ocean but once. Why only once? Jenny had wanted to know. But Mama could not, or perhaps *would* not, give her any explanation for this. So this grandfather was as much a stranger as all the others Jenny had encountered on her journey.

Would this suddenly discovered grandfather, this stranger, care for Jenny? She must give him her most winning smiles, the ones that so captivated all who had come to the dance studio, and in truth, even those many strangers she had encountered on her journey. If only her golden ringlets did not look so bedraggled. She had tried very hard, but not very successfully, to keep them looking as they had when Amah Cho Mei so lovingly cared for them.

But Jenny's grandfather, being so very rich, would have servants as well, would he not? And he would certainly wish to provide Jenny with someone to take care of her beautiful ringlets.

These thoughts did not bring her much comfort at the moment as the horses' hooves drummed relentlessly, and the carriage rolled on and on, bringing her ever closer to her final destination. She had begun to hear waves pounding on the rocks, faintly and from far in the distance, which told her she was nearly there. That was the one thing, the only thing, Mama had told her about the house: hearing the waves pounding and pounding far below it. Suddenly she drew her arms tightly around herself and shuddered. For golden ringlets and winning smiles aside, she realized that at last she was to meet this "real" grandfather she had never known she had, the father of the "real" papa she did not even remember.

Chapter II

Graymark House

The carriage came to a sudden, jolting stop. The elderly couple awoke with a start, their heads jerking up and their dim eyes darting from side to side in confusion, as if they had quite forgotten where they were. But the heavyset man threw open the carriage door and leaped out, his black cape flapping around his knees like bat wings. "Why are we stopping in this forsaken place?" he shouted angrily. "Is something wrong? And what are you doing up there with the bags? You're not touching mine, are you?"

"No, nothing wrong, sir," the driver shouted from the top of the carriage. "Just getting down the trunk and the carpetbag belonging to the young miss. This is her stop."

"Well, I wasn't advised we were going to be making any extra stops," the man snapped. "I hope this isn't going to take too long. I'm late enough as it is."

"Won't take no time at all, sir," the driver replied. "Here, Nick, give a hand with this trunk, will you?"

"Right-ee-oh," a voice sang out.

With this, the angry man climbed back into the carriage, dropping with a grunt into his seat. It seemed to matter not at all to him that he had shoved Jenny back into her seat as she tried to stand and leave the carriage. Quaking, she finally stood and managed to clamber down the steps. Her small, wood steamer trunk and carpetbag were already sitting on the ground, waiting for her. They were lit up only by the carriage lanterns, for by now the darkness of night had fallen. There were no other lights around, and the road, but for the carriage and its occupants, was otherwise deserted. But what the carriage lamp lit up, in addition to Jenny's luggage, was a narrow road with a wooden sign to one side displaying the faded words GRAYMARK HOUSE.

"Ain't there no one going to be meeting you here, miss?" the driver asked.

"I . . . I thought there was," replied Jenny, her voice quavering, for she was now truly frightened.

After all, she had believed she would be let off at a proper carriage stop, like the one at the small village they had passed through some mile or so back, complete with lamps and people on the streets. Was she to be left standing alone in the dark here in what to all intents and purposes was the middle of nowhere?

The driver pushed back his cap and scratched an ear. "You're expected, ain't you, miss?"

"Oh, yes!" Jenny cried, but then instantly gave a sharp gasp of dismay.

It had just come to her how unlikely it was that her grandfather would know the exact time of her arrival when she had had to journey such a very long way, and in several modes of transportation. Furthermore, Mama had never even received a letter from him in answer to her own. Perhaps that reply was on its way even then, but of what use was that now?

"You just remembered something, did you, miss?" the driver asked. "They ain't expecting you after all?"

"Oh, I believe they are," Jenny returned quickly, although in truth beginning to wonder if she really did believe it. "But I just did remember there wasn't any way they could have known *when* I was to arrive. And I . . . I don't even see any house here," she said, her voice beginning to quaver again. And there was no denying,

of course, that there was no house in sight, despite the sign—
nothing but a dense stand of trees, tall, dark, and threatening.

"Well, you wait here a moment, miss," the driver said, lifting a
lantern down from where it hung over his carriage seat.

As he started to walk away from the carriage, however, holding the lantern up high to light his way, the carriage door was
flung open again. "Hey, you there, driver! Where do you think
you're going? How much longer are you going to keep us waiting
here?" the heavyset man shouted.

"No longer than can be helped, sir," replied the driver.

"All right, see that that's the case," the man growled. "Otherwise I'll be talking to your employer, you may be sure of that."

"Oh, I ain't about to let that happen, sir!" the driver called back,
but his footsteps did not falter, and the sound of them quickly disappeared down the road. Minutes dragged by, but at last the footsteps
were heard returning, bringing the driver and his lantern with them.

"Just like I was thinking," he announced. "This ain't a reg'lar
road. There's two stone posts either side of it just up a ways, and a
bit farther there's house lights. Nick, give me another hand, will
you? We'll take the young miss's trunk up to the house. Think you
can manage your carpetbag, miss?"

"Oh, yes!" Jenny replied gratefully. "And thank you very much."

"No trouble, miss," the driver replied, setting his lantern down
atop Jenny's small, battered trunk. "Watch we don't knock it off!"
he warned his helper.

But the two men had no sooner picked up the trunk and
taken a few steps than the door of the cab flew open again, and an
enraged face appeared. "*Now* what's going on? If I'm five minutes
late for my appointment, you'll all pay for it. You may be sure of
that!"

"We'll get you there in good time, sir. Never you fear," the
driver returned, grimacing.

Fearful lest the man should reappear and decide to shout at *her*,

Jenny quickly picked up her carpetbag and scurried after the two carrying her trunk. For all the weight of the wood trunk, weight that came more from the trunk itself than Jenny's clothes and the few small possessions within it, the men jogged ahead rapidly, and she had to struggle to keep up with them.

The light from the bright carriage lamps was almost immediately swallowed up by the trees and dense, tall bushes. The only light now came from the small oil lantern, giving off but a tiny, faint, spectral glow as it bobbed about in the fog atop its precarious perch on the trunk carried ahead. Jenny stumbled on in the darkness, her carpetbag thumping painfully against her knees, and gravel biting into her thin-soled shoes, shoes far more fitted to flying across a smooth, shining dance floor than struggling down a dark dirt road where every step might send her crashing down onto the sharp stones.

All the while she could not help thinking how once again she was in the care of a stranger, a carriage driver whose name she did not even know but for whose kindness she would have been left standing waiting on a dark, deserted, fog-shrouded road—alone.

She had to keep telling herself over and over again that this was really just a terrible mistake. What she had thought a short while earlier must be true, that with her journey being so long, it must have been impossible for anyone to know the exact time she would arrive.

Still, should arrangements not have been made for her to be met at the station in the city? Could her grandfather not have sent his own carriage to fetch her? Surely he would have one, being so very wealthy. Perhaps he actually had sent a carriage, or perhaps even come in it himself, only to find that Jenny was not there waiting. These thoughts were quite reasonable, for of course he could not know that Mama had never received his letter in reply to her own, a letter that would have revealed the arrangements for Jenny's arrival.

How dreadful Grandfather would feel when he learned what had happened. But yet, how overjoyed he would be to see his granddaughter for the very first time, and to know that she had arrived safely at his home. So she must not think of how her feet hurt from the sharp stones, or how her knees ached from being battered by her carpetbag. She must think only of how this terrible journey would soon end when she arrived at her new, warm, bright, cheery home; of how not only would her curls be tended to, but how she would never have to carry her own heavy carpetbag again. And she must especially think of how joy would leap into Grandfather's eyes when she walked through the door.

"Here we are, miss!" the driver called out. "Here's the house, just like I said."

Intent on trying to keep from stumbling on the sharp stones, and with eyes fastened on the bobbing lantern just ahead, it was small wonder Jenny had failed to see the faint lights buried deeply in the drifts of fog. But moments later, she found herself with heart beating faster climbing the brick steps of a wide portico, its roof supported by tall, white columns. The men ahead of her quickly set down her trunk beside the massive oak door. The driver then pulled on the black iron bell chain that hung beside it. "You'll be all right now, miss," he said. "Sorry we can't wait longer." He jerked his head back in the direction of the carriage and drew a telling finger across his neck. "You get my meaning, I'm sure, miss."

Jenny nodded, for his meaning was clear indeed. "Thank you ever so much. I . . . I do hope you won't be in any trouble on my account."

"Never you fret about that," the driver said. "Good night now, miss!"

It seemed he had no sooner finished speaking than the lantern swinging from his hand disappeared into the fog and the darkness. Jenny was now alone on the dark portico. All around her there was only silence except for the sound of the waves pounding against the cliff somewhere far below the house. And where was her grandfather? Why was he not coming to the door?

At last she reached out hesitantly and tugged on the bell chain. Almost before her hand left the chain, she heard footsteps approaching. Metal scraped against metal as a bolt was pulled, and then the door swung open.

In the doorway stood an old man, his face creased and wrinkled as an ancient parchment map, topped with a sparse fringe of snow-white hair. The black coat that hung from his shoulders, thin and bent as a wire hanger, seemed to be two sizes too large for him not so much by design as that he had simply shrunk inside it. Thrusting his head forward from a too-wide collar, he held up an oil lantern to cast its light on Jenny. The flame in the lantern danced crazily in his shaking hand as he peered at her, his faded eyes blinking and blinking. But there was no trace of the joy in them that Jenny expected to see. In truth, the old man's face registered little expression of any kind.

Her heart lodged in her throat, Jenny at last managed to produce a shy smile. "Grandfather! I . . . I am Jenny!"

"Grandfather?" repeated the old man. Then suddenly his look turned hard and suspicious. His eyes narrowed warily. "What kind of prank is this? I have no grandchild. I am grandfather to no one!"

Chapter III

A Dangerous Mistake

⁂

B-B-But . . . ," Jenny stammered. "I . . . I thought . . ." The real dismay and terror she felt must have shown on her face and affected the old man, for the look on his face softened. "What you have thought, child, appears to be wrong. I tell you again, I have no grandchild."

No grandchild! How could this be?

Well, until only a few short weeks ago was it not true that Jenny had never known she had a grandfather, or at least not remembered that she had one, having been told about him when she was but a little girl? So although not easy to believe, was it not still possible that her grandfather had once known about Jenny but, not having seen or heard of her since, had forgotten all about her? After all, he did appear to be very old, and were not very old people often very forgetful?

Still, had not Jenny's mama not written him, reminding him of her existence and letting him know that she would soon be arriving? Unless—unless—"Did . . . did you not get Mama's letter?" Jenny blurted.

The old man looked puzzled. "What letter was that?"

"The one she wrote to tell you I . . . I was coming," replied Jenny, growing frightened again.

"There has been no such letter delivered here," the old man

said, frowning. "But what I'm beginning to believe is that you have come to the wrong place. Or at least that someone has brought you to the wrong place, for surely a girl of your young years could not have come so far out on her own."

The old man then raised his lamp and shone it over Jenny's head, squinting into the fog. "Whoever it is who accompanies this child, please show yourself."

"But I *have* come on my own," Jenny insisted. "Oh, the driver and his helper carried my trunk for me from the carriage, but they have now left, and there's no one out there. I've traveled all this long way by myself, indeed I have. And this is the right place. I *know* it is."

Well, had she not seen the sign that read GRAYMARK HOUSE? And was that not where she was to come? This must be the right place. It *must* be!

But the old man only shook his head again. "I'm sorry, child, but I believe the carriage driver who brought you here was given the wrong directions and has made a grievous mistake. Now, you must tell me your whole name, and perhaps it will help determine where you were really to be left off."

"My name is Jenny Bekins," Jenny replied at once, and then hesitated in confusion. "I . . . I . . . I mean, Jenny . . . Graymark!"

Jenny *Bekins!* How could she have let that slip out after all the rehearsing and rehearsing Mama had put her through to be certain that she remembered she was now to be Jenny *Graymark?* Jenny, of course, had always thought of herself as Jenny Bekins, and no one had ever corrected her when she said so. Still, she should have remembered, and when she saw the look of suspicion jump back into the old man's eyes, she knew at once how important it was for her to have remembered. Now it was too late to take back the words. Much too late!

But before the old man could speak, another voice called out harshly from a room behind him—a man's voice. "Confound it,

Crimpit, what's keeping you? Did you perish at the front door? Who's come out here on such a night at this hour? Is it Slorkin? Why aren't you bringing him in?"

As these questions were being hurled at the old man, a face suddenly peered around the door frame of the room from where the man's voice was coming. But it was the skinny face of a young boy, perhaps eleven years of age. From under a tousled, unkempt mop of straight, sandy hair tumbling over his forehead, a pair of remarkably blue eyes widened with surprise at the sight of Jenny.

"Get back here, Jingle, you scoundrel, and tend to my boots," growled the same voice. "Crimpit can handle this without any of your help."

The boy's face quickly disappeared.

"Crimpit!" shouted the voice. "Where in tarnation are you?"

"You step inside and wait right here," the old man muttered to Jenny. "I shall be right back, and we will get to the bottom of this."

Lifting up her carpetbag, Jenny stumbled over the threshold. The old man shut and firmly locked the door behind her, as if she might actually have some ideas about running off. Then, with a last warning look, he shuffled off as quickly as his spindly, old legs would carry him.

Jenny was once again left standing alone, although now in a large entry hall whose few timid, fluttering oil lamps on the walls did nothing to dispel the shadows on the high ceiling, or the deep air of gloom that filled the room. An enormous mirror set in a heavily carved gilt frame seemed hung on the wall only to reflect the images of several massive oil paintings, every one depicting scenes of angry, gray, storm-tossed ocean waves. The broad, dark staircase rising up into the shadows was guarded below by a newel post holding the head of a snarling lion. And lest this not prove warning enough, at the foot of the post lay a large, round, jet-black rug, its only design a gold dragon coiled ominously around itself, as if ready to strike.

It was hardly a room designed to dispel Jenny's feelings of dread and forboding as the same horrifying thoughts raced through her head. No letter received! The old man not her grandfather! Now he had left her standing at the door, warning that when he returned they would "get to the bottom of this."

But when they did reach the bottom, what would they find there? Would they discover that Jenny did indeed not belong in this house, and someone had made a terrible mistake? Could it have been Mama? Oh, no—impossible! For sick and frail though she had become, her mind had never dimmed. But could it be that she had somehow been misled? If so, by whom? And more frighteningly, why?

Round and round spun the questions at a dizzying speed, but all at once they came to a sudden stop as a name leaped into Jenny's head. Crimpit! That was the name called out that had summoned the old man away. And why would anyone be called away in such a manner unless they were a servant!

Oh, yes, everything was now made clear to Jenny. The old man did not believe himself to be Jenny's grandfather because, in very truth, he *was* not! He was only a servant in the household!

But someone else in that house still must be her grandfather. Was it the owner of the voice that called the old man away? It must be. Soon she would meet him. This terrible mistake would be explained away, and all questions answered. Jenny was so certain this was right, her spirits began to soar. No mistake had been made. This was the right house, after all!

With everything settled in her mind, she was able to give all her attention to the dim, cheerless room in which she found herself. What most caught her eye was the coiled dragon woven in the rug at the foot of the stairs. Must it not have come from China just as she had? After all, dragons seemed to be everywhere in China, dragons of bright red and pink paper, dragons carved on boxes of precious rosewood, dragons carved of rose quartz and jade, dragons fashioned of silver. Why, in Jenny's carpetbag at that moment was tucked away one of Mama's prized possessions, a tiny, round silver box, lined in royal blue silk, with an intricate dragon carved on its cover. The fierce dragon on the rug, far from frightening Jenny, seemed a very good sign instead.

She had little time to think further about this, however, for the old man now came shuffling back into the entry hall and beckoned to her. He continued to look at her with suspicious eyes, and did not return the timid smile she gave him. But that hardly mattered, for her thoughts were now on the grandfather she was about to meet. She could barely breathe, half from fear and half from excitement, as she picked up her carpetbag and entered the room where he awaited her.

In the room some four or five cut-glass oil lamps set on tables lit up walls lined with books reaching to the ceiling, and an enormous stone fireplace containing the glowing embers of a dying fire. Over the fireplace hung another of the oil paintings depicting the crashing, foam-flecked waves of a stormy ocean. It was viewed with magisterial indifference by a tall clock *ticktocking* the hours away in a corner of the room.

Two large red leather armchairs sat across from each other on either side of the fireplace, one of them empty. At the foot of the second chair, sitting with knees drawn up to his chin, was the owner of the boy's face that had briefly peered at Jenny through the open door. But it was the occupant of the second chair, the one facing her, who instantly captured and held her attention, making her heart beat faster. For, after all, this must finally be the person whom she had crossed an ocean and a continent to come to, the person who held the rest of her life in his hands—her grandfather!

Or—or was it?

Chapter IV

Cruel! Cruel!

𝕄

With one leg resting on a leather ottoman in front of him, the other thrown carelessly over the arm of the chair, the man lounging in the room could not have been more than thirty-six or thirty-seven years of age. Hands folded under the short, crisp, dark beard of his chin, and with one eyebrow slightly raised, he studied Jenny with piercing deep blue eyes as she entered the room.

The shy smile she was wearing trembled and then vanished entirely, for this was hardly the old man she expected to see. Still, she had so persuaded herself that it would be, that before she could think further about it, she stammered, "I . . . I am Jenny, G-G-Grandfather!"

The man continued staring, but now a twisted grin slowly appeared on his face. "Grandfather, eh? What's the saying, 'If at first you don't succeed, try, try again'? Well, it didn't work out with Crimpit, so I suppose I'm next in line to try. And you may wipe that smirk off your face, Jingle, you imp, or I'll grandfather *you*." The man paused to give the boy sitting by his chair a nudge with the toe of his boot, for which effort the boy, Jingle, merely rolled his eyes and did nothing to rearrange the expression on his face.

"In any event, my dear young girl," the man continued, "I am neither your grandfather nor any other person related to you. Now what did you say your name was?"

"Jenny G-G-Graymark," Jenny faltered, feeling her face flush. The man scowled. "No, no, no! I mean your real name," he said impatiently.

"But . . . but . . . but . . . ," began Jenny. Then, by now so confused and frightened by all the turns of events, the words froze in her throat.

"Crimpit, would you be kind enough to help the young lady out?" the man said. "She seems to have forgotten her name."

"It is my belief, Master Win," replied Crimpit, "that her name is the first one she gave me, which was Jenny Bekins."

"And that's exactly my belief as well," said the man. "For your information, Miss Jenny Bekins, my name happens to be Graymark . . . Winston Graymark IV, to be precise. As far as I know, I'm the last of the line, and no one has ever told me that there was a young girl of your age lurking in the family tree. Now what we need to know is why you were put up to this, and how you came to be on our doorstep at this ungodly hour."

"Mama wrote a letter!" Jenny blurted out. "She wrote a letter explaining everything. She *told* me she did."

"And by any chance did she also tell you about the Graymark family being very rich?" inquired Winston Graymark evenly.

Jenny hesitated only a moment before slowly nodding her head. For in very truth, was that not exactly what Mama had said when telling her what a splendid life she would have with her grandfather? Would it matter that this was only said when Mama was trying to soften the blow of revealing to Jenny that she herself would be no more?

"Why am I not surprised?" Winston Graymark said, with a telling look at Crimpit. "Well, Miss Jenny Bekins, I'm afraid that this may be a matter for the authorities."

"B-B-But Mama's letter!" Jenny pleaded in despair. "I . . . I *know* that—"

"A letter that was never received," interrupted Winston Graymark. "So what kind of story she might have invented to explain your arrival, we can now only guess. I cannot imagine, however, how she could have expected you to be accepted as a grandchild no one has ever heard of before. By the way, where is your mother now?"

"Mama is . . . Mama is no more. And . . . and both my papas are gone as well!" Jenny's voice broke in a sob.

"If that's true, then I am very sorry to hear it," said Winston Graymark. "But then who is responsible for this charade, for if your mother is no more, then she couldn't very well have written any letter, could she?"

"Mama was very ill and knew she was going to die," Jenny said. "It was then she wrote the letter to my . . . my grandfather, for there was no one else left in the world to take care of me. She told me that he was the father to my *real* papa. And that my real papa's name was . . . Cameron Graymark."

Once again, Winston Graymark folded his hands under his chin, and sat staring into the fireplace. The burning embers snapped and crackled as they sent sparks flying up the chimney. The clock *ticktocked* away relentlessly in the corner. All else in the room was silent.

At last Winston Graymark spoke, saying softly, "Cameron Graymark is my brother. When he left here, I had letters from him, but they stopped coming, and mine were returned to me unopened and marked 'address unknown.' That was nearly twelve years ago, and I have every reason to believe that he has perished.

"This is not a question of your mother knowing him, but simply that I believe no marriage ever took place between them, nor was a child ever born to them, for nothing of either event was ever mentioned by my brother in his letters to me. And doesn't it appear curious that if those two momentous events had taken place, my very own dear brother would not have reported them to me? So it appears, Miss Jenny Bekins, that your mother was married to only one man, Mr. Bekins, and you were born to them. When your mother knew that her life was drawing to an end, and her child would be left orphaned, she devised what she thought to be the clever plan of having the child pose as the long-lost grandchild of a wealthy grandparent. Alas for you, her scheme has failed."

Jenny, numbed by this horrifying turn of events, could do nothing but whisper, "But the letter . . . the letter Mama wrote. It might yet come."

"My dear young Jenny," said Winston Graymark, "even if a letter should ever come, I can promise you it will make no difference, for it would be but a tissue of lies." He paused to shake his head. "No, the truth is that you are not a member of this family, and do not belong here at all. We cannot, of course, send you out into the night alone, and you'll remain here for the night at least. We must then decide what is best done with you. Crimpit, would you please go fetch Mrs. Crimpit, and she can . . ." He stopped in midsentence, frowning. "No, no, no, what was I thinking? I'm not going to ask her to do any more stair climbing than she has to, and I expect she's retired, anyway. I'll ask Madame Dupray to handle this. Jingle, I should not have allowed you to loiter about here with your jaw hanging open minding what's none of your business. But, as I did, you may as well make yourself useful. Run upstairs, please, and summon Madame Dupray. Tell her I want her here at once."

The boy, Jingle, scrambled to his feet and ran to the doorway, casting sideways glances at Jenny. As soon as he had disappeared, Winston Graymark said, "Crimpit, take Miss Bekins's coat and bonnet. She may sit or stand as she chooses." That instruction given, he picked up a book lying on the table by his chair and began reading it as if there were no one else in the room with him.

As Crimpit laid Jenny's coat and bonnet on a table and began straightening some books on a shelf, Jenny continued standing in the same place, too stunned to make her way to any chair in the room. Or even to think. All she could do was listen to the clock *ticktocking* the minutes away forebodingly from the corner. At last, sounds were heard signaling the return of Jingle. A moment later, he entered the room followed closely by a woman.

As if knowing he might now actually be dismissed, Jingle quickly separated himself from his companion and scuttled across the room, dropping down on the same spot to which he had recently laid claim. Winston Graymark, however, did nothing but look at him and shrug, his interest now directed entirely at the woman.

Without looking right or left, she crossed the room with swift footsteps, so swift that Jenny barely caught a glimpse of a pale, thin face, and dark hair drawn back to end up severely imprisoned in a knot at the neck. The woman's stern black cotton dress was devoid of any adornment. The dress had not even a white collar and cuffs, but had instead black bands circling her neck and wrists. Her back to Jenny, she stopped before Winston Graymark, her hands folded before her. "You sent for me, Mr. Graymark?" she asked in a low voice.

"I did that, Madame Dupray," he replied. "We seem to have developed a slight problem, and I need someone to take it out of my hands until it is resolved, probably sometime tomorrow. The young girl now in the room with us has materialized on our doorstep, claiming to be a member of this family. She is not, of course."

As if she had not noticed the young girl in question, Madame Dupray slowly turned her head around and studied Jenny with curious dark eyes. "Was no one with her, Mr. Graymark?" she asked, turning back to him.

"No one," he replied.

"What is it you wish of me in this regard, Mr. Graymark?" she then asked.

"She'll need a place to stay the night," he said. "I'd like you to take her upstairs and find some spare room or other for her. You are not to mention this to . . . well, you know whom I mean. It might be disturbing."

"Of course, Mr. Graymark. I quite understand," Madame Dupray said. "But if I might be so bold as to inquire, what does one propose to do with the girl?"

Winston Graymark threw out his hands. "I really have not the remotest idea at the moment. I suppose, however, that . . . *one* simply sends her back to wherever she came from."

"She has parents, then, to whom she would go, or other relations?" asked Madame Dupray.

"None. Or so it appears," Winston Graymark replied.

"Who was it who sent her then, Mr. Graymark?" inquired Madame Dupray.

"It was the mother," he replied with some show of annoyance. "On the point of death, she wrote a letter to explain the subsequent arrival of her child, or so the girl says. I should say 'phantom letter,' however, for no such letter has ever arrived here. Not that it would have mattered if it had, for I believe there would have been not a word of truth in what the mother wrote."

"I see," said Madame Dupray. "But may I ask from what place the letter would have come? In other words, from what place did the girl come, and to what place should she be returned, Mr. Graymark?"

He shrugged and turned to Jenny. "Where *did* you come from, Miss Jenny Bekins?" he asked.

Numbed from listening to her future being settled in front of her as if she were nothing but a wood statue with no feelings, Jenny barely managed a trembling whisper. "F-F-From Ch-China."

At the sound of the word, Winston Graymark started, but quickly collected himself, and then shook his head in disbelief. "*China!* Well, I suppose if one tale can be invented, so can another equally preposterous."

Jingle, whose opinion was of course not required, gave one anyway in the form of rolling his eyes, then throwing his hand to his mouth to hide a grin.

"Excuse me, Master Win," Crimpit broke in. "But this may well be the truth, if nothing else is. Miss Bekins has with her a steamer trunk. It still sits outside the front door on the portico, but I did note that it has labels pasted on it with the name of a steamship which, I believe, plies the Pacific Ocean to the Orient."

"So it may be the truth," Winston Graymark said indifferently. "She'll have to go back anyway . . . to China or kingdom come, for all I care. She never should have been sent here in the first place."

At this, Madame Dupray gave an audible gasp, wringing her hands with dismay and disbelief. "Oh, Mr. Graymark! Surely you could not do such a thing! Why, she is only a child, and to send her back to a foreign land such as that one, where, as you have said, she has neither mother nor father nor any relations is . . . is unthinkable!"

"Friends, then," he replied coolly. "The family must have had some friends over there. Let her go to them."

"Friends?" cried Madame Dupray. "Mr. Graymark, please forgive me, for I know this is not for me to decide, but in the name of humanity, I implore you not to send the child back, across a continent and an ocean, trusting that there will be friends there who might take her in. Who knows to what fate you might be consigning her?"

"Madame Dupray," Winston Graymark said wearily, stifling a yawn. "I really did not call you down here to have your opinions on this matter. I simply wanted you to find a place to keep the girl until morning. But, all right, since you have expressed an opinion, perhaps you would have one on what should be done with her if she is not sent back."

"You refuse to allow her to stay here, Mr. Graymark?" Madame Dupray asked.

"Why in heaven's name should I?" he replied. "She is not a member of the family."

Madame Dupray hesitated. "Would you consider, then, allowing her to stay not as a member of the family, or even as a guest, but . . . but perhaps as a servant? I believe I understood you to say that another helper for Mrs. Crimpit, being aged, would not be amiss in the kitchen, or to assist Lilly."

Winston Graymark looked at her sharply. "May I ask, Madame Dupray, why you have so much interest in what happens to this girl?"

"My . . . my own past causes me to have great sympathy for her situation, Mr. Graymark," she replied haltingly.

"All right, then. Although it is against my better judgment, I'll allow it," he said, turning to Jenny. "Miss Bekins, it seems you now have two choices . . . return to China, if it really is your former home, or stay here as a servant. So which will it be?"

Two choices? One to make the long journey back across the continent and then another longer, terrible passage across the ocean—to what? To friends, it was suggested. But Jenny knew there were no friends to take her in. And she could well guess that being patted on the head for winning smiles and golden ringlets by visitors to the dance studio did not mean someone would wish to take you home with them as their own.

Winston Graymark was wrong. Jenny had but one choice. Only one! It was to remain as a servant and wait on others as she had always been waited on—to see all her mama's dreams for her turn to ashes.

"I . . . I would like to stay," she replied in a barely heard whisper.

"So be it," said Winston Graymark. "Madame Dupray, you will now, of course, refrain from finding a room for Jenny upstairs, but will see that you find her a place in the servants' quarters. Make any other arrangements that you see fit. I want no more to do with it."

Without another glance at Jenny, he abruptly rose from his

chair. This act, however, was not accomplished without some effort, for, as could now be seen, he was crippled with a misshapen back and hip, causing him to list to one side when he finally stood up. "Confound it, Jingle," he barked. "Don't just sit there gaping. Hand me my cane. And while you're at it, take this book and bring it along."

Silently, Madame Dupray and Crimpit stepped to one side as he limped heavily to the doorway. But at the door, he paused. "Madame Dupray, do something about that outrageous dress she's wearing, and those ridiculous curls. I can't stand the sight of either."

"Ridiculous curls"! "Outrageous," the pink satin dress chosen especially to please her grandfather! After all these past weeks of misery, this last was, finally, too much for her to bear. Jenny hung her head, fighting to hold back the tears.

And then she heard the words, words spoken so softly, it was certain they were intended for her ears alone. "Cruel! Cruel!"

She raised her head slowly, and found herself looking into the dark eyes of Madame Dupray.

Chapter V

Dire Warnings

※

I f there was any look of pity on Madame Dupray's face, it must have come and gone in an instant, for Jenny never saw it as Madame Dupray turned to look nervously over her shoulder at Crimpit, now starting to turn down the oil lamps in the room.

"Fetch your coat and bonnet and come with me at once," she said in a taut voice as she turned back to Jenny. "Someone will see to your trunk in the morning. But you must carry your carpetbag yourself and not expect Mr. Crimpit to do it for you. You are a servant now, Jenny. I trust you will remember that."

Madame Dupray continued throwing guarded looks over her shoulder at Crimpit all the while she was speaking, and did not lower her voice in the slightest. It appeared that she actually wished to have all that she said to Jenny heard by him.

Her face without expression, the look in her eyes distant, she waited while Jenny struggled with her coat and bonnet, then turned abruptly and walked swiftly from the room without another glance at her.

Was it not but a short while ago that Jenny had told herself that never again would she have to carry a heavy carpetbag? Now Jenny Bekins—who was never to be Jenny Graymark, destined to charm a grandfather with winning smiles and bouncing ringlets—Jenny Bekins, servant girl, leaned over to wrap her small, still-aching fingers around the handle of the carpetbag, and went trudging to the door. By now, the last lamp was being turned down, and but for a faint glimmer from the embers in the fireplace, the room was plunged in darkness. Like Jenny's past, it seemed to have vanished.

"Cruel! Cruel!" How true those words were! But could they actually have come from the owner of the figure gliding ahead of Jenny, a stiff, stern pillar of funereal black, one that never turned once to look back to offer even a faint smile or look of encouragement?

If only Madame Dupray would turn to her once. But she did not. They paraded on in silence. The only sounds heard were their footsteps, the *thump-thump* of the carpetbag against Jenny's knees, and the *shuffle-shuffle* of Crimpit following somewhere behind them.

Leaving the hall, Madame Dupray led Jenny into a large, handsomely furnished room lit only by a pair of oil lamps palely fluttering on each side of a wide, bronze-framed mirror. The mirror hung over an imposing silver tea service and candelabra displayed on a massive sideboard, and reflected a long mahogany dining table with a dozen richly carved chairs in attendance. But as with the hall now left behind, the room wore an air of gloom, deepened not only by the tarnish that dulled the silver, and the pall of dust that lay on the furniture, but by the now-familiar paintings. There were four of these hulking paintings of stormy oceans hurling angry foam into the air as they faced each other in rage across the table. Jenny quickly looked away from them, for while earlier she had given little thought to such scenes, now for some reason they sent a shiver up her spine.

From this bleak room she was led, thumping and bumping, into a pantry whose only light came through the doorway from the room beyond. The room proved to be the kitchen, marked by the requisite black iron coal stove planted stolidly in one corner; iron sink and array of pots and pans and other instruments of cooking; and at the center of the room a large, well-worn pine worktable. Although no signs of food preparation remained in the room, it was, unlike the dining room, occupied by two people.

One was a small, gray-haired woman enveloped in an over-sized white muslin apron and preoccupied at that moment in lift-ing a plate of biscuits from a cupboard. The second occupant of the room was a girl of perhaps eighteen or nineteen years of age. She was seated with an elbow on the table beside a teacup and saucer, her hand propping up her chin. With her other hand she was toying with tattered bits of buttered bread on the dish in front of her. The girl was in a dress remarkably similar to that worn by Madame Dupray, stark black without a touch of any ornamenta-tion. Even her dark hair was drawn back in the same severe man-ner, ending in a knot tightly twisted at her neck.

At the sound of footsteps entering the kitchen, the girl turned her head sharply, staring. The old woman, taking slightly longer to register the arrivals, then thrust her neck forward to peer at them through a pair of bird-sized wire spectacles.

Madame Dupray finally stopped, waiting a brief moment for Jenny to come thumping up beside her. "Mrs. Crimpit," she said, addressing the old woman with the barest nod of her head in Jenny's direction. "This is Jenny . . . Jenny Bekins."

"Eh? What was that?" the old woman said, holding a hand up to her ear.

"This is Jenny Bekins," Madame Dupray repeated in a louder voice. "Jenny is an orphan whom Mr. Graymark has kindly agreed to keep here as a servant, for she had no place to go. She may help you in any way that you and Mr. Crimpit see fit, perhaps in assist-ing Lilly."

"That will be very nice, I'm sure," said Mrs. Crimpit with a dim smile. "Lilly would like the help."

Would she? Well, if Lilly was the girl sitting at the table, as Jenny believed her to be, it was not hard to imagine from the cool look of appraisal she fastened on Jenny just how much she would like to have anything to do with a mere child such as Jenny was. Worse, a mere child with "ridiculous" golden ringlets, and an "outrageous" dress of bright pink satin replete with bows, lace, and red rosebuds. Jenny had little doubt that producing her winning smile for the benefit of this girl with straight, dark hair shackled to her head, and wearing a dismal black dress unadorned by so much as one colored button, would have done no more good than it had done with Winston Graymark. Probably less!

But as Jenny stood helplessly, wondering what was to happen to her next, she was startled to hear Madame Dupray say in a low voice, "Violet, I believe the room next to yours is not in use. Isn't that so?"

Violet! So this was not the Lilly whom Jenny was to assist after all. Still, how was Violet to take Jenny's occupying a room right next to hers? The swiftness of Violet's reply answered the question at once. "But the room *is* in use," she said without so much as drawing a breath. "Lilly uses it to . . . to rest when she needs to."

"Then Lilly will have to *rest* elsewhere," snapped Madame Dupray.

"Well . . .well, what if Mr. and Mrs. Crimpit don't like it?" Violet said, no small hint of rebellion in her voice.

"You will let me deal with that," replied Madame Dupray, silencing Violet with a long, hard look. "And you had better finish what you are about, for I wish you to return upstairs. I shall be up again shortly. Mrs. Crimpit, if you have no objection," she continued, raising her voice and speaking so slowly and carefully, it almost seemed as if she considered Mrs. Crimpit to be not only deaf but dimwitted as well, "I will give Jenny the room next to Violet's, and will take her there now. Would that be satisfactory to you?"

"Oh, that . . . that will be fine, I'm sure," replied Mrs. Crimpit so uncertainly, it almost did seem that the matter was too much for her to deal with.

Without further notice of Mrs. Crimpit or Violet, who had already begun fiddling with her bits of bread and butter and was now ignoring Jenny's presence entirely, Madame Dupray swept from the room, with Jenny once again following, thumping and bumping after her.

Instead of continuing down the passageway leading from the kitchen, however, Madame Dupray made a sharp turn and led Jenny down a steep, narrow flight of steps. And with each treacherous step, Jenny's heart sank further and further, for there was little doubt that, as a servant, this is where she would be expected to live—in a cellar!

At the foot of the steps they were met by only a single oil lamp, its tiny yellow eye staring at them unblinking in the dank, dead cellar air. It offered but feeble help in lighting the passageway that branched in both directions. In near darkness, Jenny stumbled after Madame Dupray, who moved swiftly and surely down one passage, silent except to point out tersely the washroom and the room that belonged to Violet. Turning into the next room, she drew a matchbox from her skirt pocket. Shielding a fluttering match flame with her hand, she crossed the room to light a tin oil lamp sitting on a small chest of drawers.

The little flame that flared up in the lamp was enough to show Jenny all there was to see in the tiny room—a narrow iron cot, the chest of drawers, and a straight-backed wooden chair. All were painted a nondescript brown. On the wall, a row of nails appeared to be all there was by way of a wardrobe, while over the chest hung something in an oval frame so dulled and spotted, any resident of the room would have been hard put to call it a mirror.

There was no sign of any bit of carpet on the floor, any pillow on the bone-hard chair, or curtain at the small window—a window, it might be added, placed so high in the wall that any view through it could only be found by first climbing on the chair.

Jenny's attention, however, was almost immediately drawn away from this bleak little room by the sight of Madame Dupray creeping back to the doorway. There she peered cautiously out in the passageway, and then stealthily shut the door behind her. Her face, when she turned back to Jenny, was taut. Her eyes darted nervously around the room. Indeed, Madame Dupray gave every sign of being truly frightened!

Her heart beating faster, Jenny set down her carpetbag and waited for Madame Dupray to speak.

"Jenny, what you heard me say to you, and only you, in the library, was what I felt," Madame Dupray said. "It was cruel and unthinkable to have such things said to you, a child newly orphaned."

"Oh, thank you for your kindliness!" cried Jenny, overcome in knowing that those words—"Cruel! Cruel!"—had been truly meant.

"Sadly," Madame Dupray continued, "what I must tell you *now* is that what I said, or may feel, is of no import whatsoever. I have been hired to oversee the care of someone related to Mr. Graymark, and though it may appear that I have some standing in this household, make no mistake about it: I am but a servant just as you are. Worse, this may be the last time I will be able to talk to you freely as I am doing now. We must from this time on be but strangers to each other!"

"S-S-Strangers?" stammered Jenny. "But, why?"

"Because," replied Madame Dupray, "having spoken up in your behalf, I will be closely watched in my dealings with you by those who are greatly favored here." She paused, lowering her voice. "Did you note those doors ahead of us just as we turned to come down the steps to the cellar?"

Jenny nodded. She had indeed noted those doors, thinking that that was where her room lay. Instead, she had been led to a cellar!

"Those doors," continued Madame Dupray, "lead to the

rooms occupied by Mr. and Mrs. Crimpit. First-floor rooms, Jenny, not rooms in the cellar, where you and Violet must live. Mr. and Mrs. Crimpit have been retainers in this household since before the birth of Mr. Graymark, and they are the favored ones. And you must not be fooled by them, for nice, old people as they appear to be, they are still crafty. And they have Mr. Graymark's ear, Jenny. You must never forget that. Never!"

Madame Dupray then clasped her hands together tightly in an agitated manner, looking intently into Jenny's eyes. "Now there is one more thing you must *never* forget, something more important than all else. If you do, it may cause me great grief. You see, my job as servant here is to tend to the needs of one person. That person is Mr. Graymark's father."

Winston Graymark's father! Was that not, then, Cameron Graymark's father as well? Someone who was to have been Jenny's grandfather in that very house after all! Jenny gave a sharp gasp.

This was not missed by Madame Dupray. "What is it, Jenny?" she asked quickly. "What is the matter?"

"Oh, Madame Dupray!" cried Jenny, a sob caught in her throat. "That . . . that is the person I believed was my . . . my grandfather!"

"So that was your claim to this family," said Madame Dupray softly. "And now Mr. Winston Graymark says you have no such claim. All your hopes and expectations so cruelly ended by him. But, sadly, such terrible things happen to us all, and you must try to be brave and deal with what life hands you, just as I have done, and must do. And here now, for me, is one of those things. I must order you never to enter old Mr. Graymark's room at the far end of the upstairs gallery, the room directly next to my own, unless I am there, or is my assistant, Violet. You see, Mr. Graymark is grown accustomed to us, but becomes very disturbed if any others, excepting his son, are there without one of us present."

"Even Mr. and Mrs. Crimpit?" asked Jenny.

"Even them," said Madame Dupray. "But it is you for whom I

am largely responsible, as you are here at my request. It would go badly with me if you were the cause of any difficulties. So you must absolutely promise to remember this warning. Will you, Jenny?"

"Yes, oh yes, I do promise! I will remember, Madame Dupray!" breathed Jenny fervently.

"I devoutly pray that you do!" replied Madame Dupray, a pale, slender hand pressed to her heart. "But before I leave you, we must tend to your dress and your curls, and we must do it quickly. Let me see what is in your carpetbag that might be better than your present dress."

Jenny instantly lifted her carpetbag and set in on the cot. But before she could open it, Madame Dupray anxiously pushed her to one side. "Here, I will help you with this, for time is running out, and I must hurry back upstairs. I *must* hurry!"

With nervous, shaking fingers, she unbuckled the leather straps and began swiftly snatching out the contents of the carpetbag. It took her only moments to have everything in it strewn across the cot. Seemingly not content, however, that everything *had* been taken out, she continued to rummage in the carpetbag, going deep into the pockets that lined it.

"Oh!" she exclaimed, holding up a small object she had found in the depths of a pocket. "What is this? Why, I see it is a pretty little silver box with a dragon embossed on it. May I open it?" she asked eagerly, raising the lid of the box before Jenny could even reply.

"It belonged to Mama," Jenny said shyly. "The bit of hair tied with the pink ribbon is mine from when I was a baby."

"I suspected so," said Madame Dupray, handing Jenny the box. "And as I also suspect this is a very precious article to you, I would like to warn you to keep it well hidden in your room. I have cautioned you about Mr. and Mrs. Crimpit. They are jealously suspicious of all that goes on in this house. I even have reason to believe that my own room is . . . is *searched* from time to time.

But"—she darted a nervous glance over her shoulder at the window—"but I must say no more about this."

She now began to rifle through the small heap of clothing that lay on the cot, and finally held up one of the three dresses that she found there. The dress was of a deep purple silk, but while hardly plain, it was far less decorated with lace and ribbons than the one Jenny wore.

"This will have to do, I'm afraid," Madame Dupray said, shaking her head with a worried frown. "But now we must tend to your curls."

Within moments, it was all over. *Snip! Snip! Snip!* With a small pair of scissors drawn from her pocket, Madame Dupray had done her work. Jenny's ringlets, the ones that were destined to charm her grandfather, and which a servant was to care for lovingly, now lay in sad little tangled heaps on the cold brick floor. And Madame Dupray did not even have the time to stay and mourn the loss with Jenny. One quick look at her pocket watch, and she rushed to the door.

"I must go now. I cannot wait here longer," she cried softly. "But remember, remember well . . . from now on we must meet only as strangers. If, however, you must deliver any message to me, you may do it through Violet. She is to be trusted. But no one else . . . no one else! And now, Jenny, I bid you good-bye!"

Without so much as a faint smile or single further word of comfort, Madame Dupray was gone, with only her words of warning left to tremble in the air behind her. Jenny Bekins, servant girl, was now left standing alone in her cellar room with thoughts almost too much to be borne. For it appeared that her one hope of a friend in that great, gloomy house had been handed to her only to be instantly snatched away.

Not even a sweet "good night" at the door, but a cold "good-bye." Oh, yes, there was no doubt, Madame Dupray had already become nothing but a stranger!

Chapter VI

A Puzzling Late-Night Conversation

⚕

After the door gave notice of Madame Dupray's departure with its unmistakable final click, Jenny continued to stand, frozen, in the middle of the room. Then all at once she threw her arms around herself and squeezed her eyes tightly shut. If only she could open them and find this nightmare suddenly ended!

If only she could open her eyes and find herself back in her own familiar room with her loving amah turning back her coverlets, and Mama coming in soon to bid her good night. But this wish was of no use, and when she opened her eyes, she was still alone in a chilling little cellar room, with clothes piled in disarray on a narrow iron cot. Clearly, there would be no one to help her with anything. Whatever had to be done, she must do herself. First she must find a safe hiding place for the treasured silver box she still held in her hand. And where in that barren little room was such a place to be found?

She finally decided that the only hiding place was under the thin mattress on the cot. Quickly, she slid the box under it, all the while remembering the nervous glance Madame Dupray had cast over her shoulder at the window. But Jenny determined she must not allow herself to think about that small, dark bit of glass with no curtain over it. After a hurried trip down the dark passageway to the washroom, from which she returned with hands stinging from an encounter with the ice-cold water, she quickly set about putting away the few things that had been held by her carpetbag.

As she was doing so, she tried to keep her eyes away from that dark little window high in the wall. And just as diligently she tried to keep from looking into the mirror over the chest. In the end, this turned out to be impossible, and she found herself staring into the dulled and spotted image of a waif with a sunken face made ghostly pale from weariness and misery. And where had hung sunny, golden ringlets, there was nothing left but untidy, scraggly wisps of hair. It was a face Jenny hardly recognized as hers. It was, in terrible truth, the face of yet another stranger!

As she gazed at the strange face, trying to make herself believe it was really hers, she saw tears rolling down the cheeks, and knew that this time they were real. They were not just the reflection of rain drizzling down a carriage window. And who was there to say she had no right to shed them now? For she knew that the face in the mirror belonged to a young girl doomed to live as a servant in a chilling, dank room in a cellar. And there was no one left in the world to care.

Gulping down the tears, Jenny pulled off her dress, the pink satin dress once so loved and now to be held in such contempt, and climbed into her nightdress. Lantern in hand, she threaded her way around the clumps that were once her ringlets, lying lifeless on the rough brick floor. Setting the lantern down by her cot, she climbed in, leaned over, and turned off the flame. And immediately wished she had left it on as the deep darkness wrapped itself around her.

In the darkness she realized something she had not sensed before: that even though muffled by the thick cellar walls, there could be heard the crashing of ocean waves against the cliff somewhere far below the house. Immediately she saw in her mind the paintings of a cruel and angry ocean that hung everywhere in that gloomy house. She pulled her coverlet up over her head, but could not drown out the sound.

Oh, how could she bear to remain here? Why not just run away? But she had no sooner had this thought than the memory came back to her of how she had felt when, for a few brief moments, she had thought she might be abandoned by the roadside in the dark after her carriage ride ended.

Besides, where would she run? And, more importantly, to whom? If nobody wanted her with ringlets and winning smiles, who would want the straggly waif she had become? A mangy, flea-infested old alley cat had as much chance of finding a home as she did. So it seemed she had only one choice, the exact same one she had had earlier, and that was to stay. Stay to be a servant in this great, grim house, where no one much cared if she lived or died, and to live in this tiny, dank room in the cellar, listening every night to the angry waves crashing against the cliff.

Crashing! Crashing! Crashing! It was the ceaseless sound Jenny heard as she lay in her cot, and kept hearing until her weary eyes finally closed, and she was asleep.

Jenny awoke with a start, her heart pounding. It was still dark outside her window, so she knew it was not yet daybreak. She also felt she had not been asleep for very long. What had awakened her was a terrible dream. In it she had been running through a deep fog, trying to catch up with a shadow she could see hurrying just ahead of her. The shadow belonged to her mama. Then it was swallowed up by the fog, but Jenny kept running and running after it, beginning to sob as she ran. It was the sound of her own sobbing that had awakened her. Or so she thought for a few moments, until she realized the sound came from someplace else and had then become part of her dream.

The sobbing continued. It was coming through the wall directly behind the head of her cot, a heart-wrenching sound that somehow filled her with dread. And the wall was the one that separated her from Violet's room!

Then Jenny heard the muffled sound of a woman's voice speaking. The sobbing grew louder, and the voice sharpened. Jenny heard the words "you will awaken . . . ," and the sobbing quieted down.

More muffled words were spoken, which she could not make out, and the sobbing started up again, rising to a new pitch. This was followed by an even sharper warning: "Stop it! Stop it! How would you like to be in the cellar forever? Think about it! It is no use. . . ." The woman's voice then lowered again, so no further words could be understood. But the sobbing stopped, and at last Jenny heard the sound of a door closing, signaling that someone had left the room.

Only moments later, Jenny heard her own door open. She snapped her eyes shut, keeping them tightly closed as footsteps quietly crossed the room. They stopped at her cot, and she felt the warmth of an oil lantern being held over her face. Then the footsteps returned to the door. Opening her eyelids to allow in only the tiniest sliver of light, Jenny was able to see the back of the person now disappearing through the doorway. It was the same back whose owner she had seen standing so rigidly before Winston Graymark in the library. It was the back belonging to Madame Dupray!

And so it must have been Madame Dupray who was speaking in Violet's room. And it must have been Violet sobbing. But, why? What had Madame Dupray been saying to her to cause such an outburst? Jenny tried to remember the few words she had heard, and guess their meaning. "You will awaken" and "Stop it!" were clear enough. Madame Dupray did not wish anyone in the house to be disturbed, especially Jenny, who was in the very next room.

But did those other words that she had heard not refer especially to her as well? "How would you like to be in the cellar forever?" Were those not almost the same words Jenny had said to herself earlier that night?

Could Madame Dupray, who felt such a deep sympathy for

Jenny's plight, have noted the dislike with which Violet had looked at Jenny, and come to reprimand her for it? It hardly seemed possible that this could have brought such a violent outburst. But from what Jenny had seen take place in the kitchen, it was clear that Violet did not like taking orders from Madame Dupray. So being called to task for her behavior might well have brought on the sobs of rebellion, especially if she were now being ordered to be nice to Jenny, to whom she appeared to have taken an instant dislike.

And *this* was the only person who was to be trusted to speak for Jenny to Madame Dupray! Despite all her efforts to hold them back, tears again rolled down Jenny's cheeks. But she knew they must be silent tears. For Violet must never know how easily sounds carried through the walls, or that Jenny had been awake to hear Madame Dupray. If so, how terrible might Violet's feelings be toward her? Oh, yes, Jenny's room must remain silent that night. Very silent indeed!

Chapter VII

Lilly's Lessons in What's What

⁂

Although Jenny was certain she could not drop off to sleep again after what had just befallen, she did at last. And when she next awoke, it was to see that the faintest light of dawn had replaced the darkness outside her window. This time what had awakened her was a sharp, impatient knock on her door. The door then immediately flew open, before she could even gather her wits together to reply to the knock.

Standing in the doorway, holding an oil lantern, was a girl perhaps the age of Violet. The light from the lantern fluttered over a freckled, ruddy-cheeked face as flat as a dinner plate. Set on it were a small, pointy nose, a mouth wide as a butter dish, and bleached blue eyes that seemed to be permanently fixed in the shape of wide, startled O's. This was all topped by what appeared at first to be a bowl decorated with odd orange spikes but then revealed itself to be simply hair done up in a great quantity of paper curlers.

After fixing Jenny with her pale eyes in a curiously indifferent stare, this apparition, encased in a gray muslin apron, marched over to the dresser, set down her lantern, and drew from her pocket a large square of white muslin. This she proceeded to fold and tie around her head so efficiently that the only remaining evidence of the curlers was the field of scattered lumps sprouting under her head scarf. The girl then proceeded to stand before the mirror, primping away little wisps of hair, and unashamedly admiring her image.

"I'm Lilly," she volunteered at last. "I've been told you're Jenny, and you're to help me with the chores. Won't be for long, you might as well know. They ain't been told yet, but I'm to be wed, and I ain't got intentions of wasting my time here much longer. Soon I'll be able to wear my hair curly as you please without tying it all up. Your hair's a mess, if you'll excuse me saying so," Lilly continued, talking to Jenny via her reflection in the mirror. "Looks like you might of cut it yourself. Did they make you do it?"

"Y-Y-Yes," stammered Jenny, never before having met up with anyone so outspoken. "But someone else cut it," she hastened to add.

"Well, whoever done it made a mess, anyway. Pity for you. You should of just wore a 'kerchief like me. You might of spoke up about it. How old are you, anyway?" Lilly asked.

"Eleven," replied Jenny, who was still perched on the edge of her cot. She was not certain if she should begin to dress, or wait for Lilly to finish primping and leave.

But Lilly did not seem to be in any hurry to go anywhere. "Hmmmmph," she sniffed. "Pity for you again. I didn't get sent into service until I was twelve, Ma saying I didn't know what was what and all until then. Started out as a helper, like you. But maybe you won't be a helper for long. Ain't a body in the village what I know of wants to come up here to work. Looks like it might be just you, 'lest that boy gets to do more than just mess about in the stable. Well, none of my business now. Hey, what's this? This your dress?" Lilly began fingering one of Jenny's dresses hanging on the wall. Her eyebrows flew up her forehead as she discovered the material the dress was made of. Then she fingered the dresses beside it.

"You going to go working in *these?*" she asked, her pale eyes all but popping right out of her head. "They'll be ruint. Ain't you got another dress for service?"

Jenny shook her head. "All my dresses are just like these."

"*All?*" Lilly's eyes popped even further. "You mean you got more someplace?"

"In my trunk. It hasn't been brought to my room yet," replied Jenny.

The look on Lilly's flat face changed instantly. She looked slyly at Jenny. "You ain't got one or two to spare, have you? You're only a portion of my size, but Ma sews and could make something of it for me. Did I tell you I was going to be wed? You ain't got any use in service for lots more dresses like these. If you wished to give me a dress or two for a wedding gift, it wouldn't go amiss with me."

Although Jenny had begun to think that nothing this Lilly could say or do would be surprising, she was so taken aback by this brazen request from someone she had just met that she could not even open her mouth to reply.

"Oh, well, just think about it," said Lilly breezily. "Anyways, I'm off now. After we've et, I'll be taking you around, showing you what's what. But you best get yourself dressed in a hurry. You been sitting round resting yourself long enough, seems to me."

Jenny, of course, had only been sitting around "resting" herself because she had been too polite to interrupt Lilly. But that seemed to concern Lilly not at all as she went flouncing out of the room, taking her lantern with her. Fortunately, enough light now came through the little window that Jenny did not have to stumble about finding a match for her own lantern as she hurriedly began to dress. But she had no more than pulled over her head the purple silk dress chosen by Madame Dupray than the door flew open, and in came Lilly again.

"All but forgot. Mrs. Crimpit's near out of coal for the stove. You might's well learn about coal getting while you're at it. Too bad 'bout that silk dress being ruint, 'specially when there's lots better uses for it." Lilly threw her chin up in the air with a sniff at this observation.

After Jenny made a quick stop at the washroom, for which Lilly let it be known by the look on her face that she was being deeply imposed upon, they arrived at the coal room further down the cellar corridor. There Jenny soon learned what was meant by Lilly's definition of "what's what." It simply meant Lilly standing about examining her fingernails while Jenny did all the work. "You ain't going to learn a thing not doing it yourself," explained Lilly.

How much teaching was required to shovel and fill a bucket of coal, Jenny failed to see. She did not think, however, it would avail her anything to mention this. The only actual help from Lilly came when she wrapped her hand around the handle of the bucket just as Jenny, having struggled up the stairs with it, entered the kitchen, thus making it look as if Lilly had had a hand in the whole operation.

Not that anybody in the kitchen appeared to care very much. They were Mr. and Mrs. Crimpit, and Violet. Violet, her eyes still suspiciously red rimmed, was sitting at the kitchen table finishing her breakfast. She looked up, hesitated a moment, and then managed to give Jenny a thin smile. Once she had got this out of the way, however, she gave Lilly a telling glance, a glance that Jenny could not fail to note. The thought that these two might be friends, unlikely as it seemed, somehow gave Jenny a sinking feeling.

Mrs. Crimpit, at the other end of the kitchen table, was totally absorbed in filling two trays with food—dishes of sliced apples, bowls of hot porridge, pitchers of cream, small bowls of sugar, muffins, rashers of sizzling bacon, eggs newly lifted from a pot of water bubbling on the stove, and cups of tea. The trays were no sooner filled than Violet quickly pushed herself away from the table and hurried from the kitchen carrying the larger of the two trays. Mrs. Crimpit then lifted two eggs from a second pot of boiling water and laid them tenderly on the second, smaller tray.

"You tell Master Win they're just the way he likes them, harder than any rocks," she said.

"As so you've been telling him for night these dozens of years," replied Mr. Crimpit with a deep sigh. "I expect he knows it by now." Shaking his head over the tray, he picked it up and shuffled with it from the room.

Mrs. Crimpit then set on the table a bowl of apples, and two plates, each containing a muffin and an egg, while Lilly sauntered over to the stove and filled two cups with tea.

"If you'd like more, there's more, Jenny," Mrs. Crimpit said, smiling absently over her shoulder as she removed her apron and hung it up on a wall peg. "Lilly, if you don't mind, the frying pan *does* need special attention. Thank you, dear!" Another dim smile further creased her wrinkled face as she left for the rooms where, Jenny had now learned, she lived with Mr. Crimpit.

"Well, eat up!" said Lilly, plopping herself down in a chair with a *thump*. "We got all them pots and pans to do up before the rest of the house." She had no sooner finished speaking than she began stuffing her mouth with large bites of muffin. And before Jenny had made it halfway through her own, Lilly was up and at the kitchen counter helping herself to a second.

But Jenny had learned that, if nothing else, there was at least one good thing about her new life at Graymark House. It was that, even though a meal might not be served with style, the servants were well fed, even the lowliest ones such as herself and Lilly. Nevertheless, when the meal was over, Jenny was to learn something more in keeping with what had gone before. It was that Lilly's ideas of showing her "what's what" extended from the coal cellar to the kitchen sink.

Therefore, Jenny ended up standing before a mountain made up of pots, baking tins, mixing bowls, spoons, and a great black, greasy frying pan. Lilly, meanwhile, remained at the table sipping her tea and telling Jenny what was what about the art of dish-washing.

"Watch you don't get water splashed on the floor," warned

Lilly. "You ain't going to get anything clean 'lest you rub with soap. And remember what Mrs. Crimpit said 'bout that frying pan needing special attention." Lilly leaned back and stared dreamily at the ceiling. "Soon it won't be me standing at that sink anymore. I'm to be wed, you know. Jed's his name. He's right-hand man to Mr. Clampett, the blacksmith," she concluded proudly.

Jenny at eleven had not much experience with the world, but it did seem to her that an assistant to a blacksmith might not be the loftiest position one could hold, and that while Lilly might not be standing at that particular sink, she would surely be standing at some sink, probably for the rest of her days.

Jenny did not believe Lilly would welcome this opinion from her, and she was too polite to have said it, anyway. Besides, it was difficult to be concerned about Lilly's future wedded bliss when at the moment her arms had begun to ache, her hands were already red and raw from the strong cake of yellow soap she must rub on the pans, and she had yet to face the dreaded black frying pan that needed so much special attention.

By the time this was all done, Jenny was quite ready to return to the cellar, where, aching, sore, and miserable, she could fall into her cot. And then Lilly announced cheerfully that they were not yet finished in the kitchen, for they—meaning Jenny, there was little doubt—would later do the dishes that would be brought back on the trays. When they did finally ever get back to the cellar, it would be for Jenny to learn what was what about doing the laundry. In the meantime, they—Jenny, again, of course—had the rest of the house to "do." So once Lilly had grudgingly passed on Jenny's pot-and-pan work, the two of them, armed with dust cloths, brooms, dustpans, and mops, set out from the kitchen.

Chapter VIII

Ghosts in the Gallery

⟨⟩

Although it was daylight, a heavy fog still roiled against the dining-room windows, casting a gray pall over the massive table and chairs hulking in the middle of the room, and the foreboding paintings of furious, foam-flecked oceans glaring down on them.

"Spooky, ain't it?" commented Lilly. "'Course it ain't any worse'n the rest of this place. It ain't a wonder that no girls in the village has a interest to go into service here. *I* might never of, except Ma said I wasn't to be so silly and turn down what pays lots more than most. But good thing I'm to be wed, is all I can say. Too bad for Violet. What chance does she got to be wed, 'long as she's here, I ask you? Or you, neither, come to think on it."

Needless to say, among the list of horrors that had befallen Jenny, her matrimonial prospects, or lack of them, had not yet appeared. So she really could come up with no suitable reply to Lilly's question. She did, however, have a question of her own as Lilly went stumping across the room without stopping.

"Shouldn't we dust the furniture here?" she asked.

Lilly's pale eyes widened. "Whatever for? It was done no more'n three weeks ago, and nobody eats here but Mr. Graymark, the young one, that is. He's never one to complain about a bit of dust, not to the Crimpits, anyways. Trays for the old gent and madam get carried upstairs, if you noted."

Lilly stopped suddenly to primp in the dining-room mirror, almost causing Jenny to crash right into her. "You might have a interest in knowing," she went on, "as how up till a year and a half ago, Mr. Crimpit waited on young Mr. Graymark, and Mrs. Crimpit done all this work. I was just helper to Mrs. Crimpit. When the old gent got his stroke, Mrs. Crimpit waited on him, with me taking on the rest. Mrs. Crimpit said she weren't surprised about the stroke, considering how the old gent started fading way back when it looked as if the younger Mr. Graymark were never coming back. Anyways, when waiting on the old gent got too much for Mrs. Crimpit, then's when madam got hired. After that, Mr. Graymark got hisself Jingle 'stead of Mr. Crimpit."

"Where . . . where did Madame Dupray come from?" asked Jenny as they started up again, hoping that with all Lilly's knowledge, she might have some notion of Madame Dupray's mysterious past.

"Beats me," said Lilly. "All I know's she keeps a sharp eye on the old gent, and got Mr. Graymark thinking she knows what's best for his pa, the poor old thing. But it's no never mind to me, nor you, neither. All you got to worry 'bout is what I already told you. If nobody gets found in the village to come work here, which is more 'n likely, then you'll be on your own, just like me."

"Doing the whole house by myself?" breathed Jenny.

"That's right!" said Lilly. "Which now tells you why I pay no never mind to the dining room. Nor much else excepting madam's and the old gent's and Mr. Graymark's rooms, and the library, which he lives in mostly."

"But . . . but don't Mr. and Mrs. Crimpit mind about how everything looks?" asked Jenny.

Lilly shrugged. "The Crimpits is been turning blind as bats, or more nearly as blind. Too old by half to be in service, if you ask me. But I expect Mr. Graymark'll keep them on till they fall over dead. Anyways, shouldn't be anything to you how old the Crimpits is getting. The older the better, I say, on account of what they don't see, they don't ask you to do. So I mostly do what suits my fancy. If you're smart, you'll do the same."

By the time Lilly had finished this speech, they had crossed the hall and entered a large room elegantly furnished with a Persian carpet, gleaming mahogany tables and side chairs, and several chairs richly upholstered in velvet and damask. A pair of gold-framed mirrors hung to the right and the left of the windows at the far side of the room, but on the rest of the walls, with one or two exceptions, hung more of the grim oil paintings of ocean waves, by now already familiar to Jenny.

"This is the parlor," Lilly announced, as if it needed explaining. "Seems I just done it a week or so ago. But, oh well, I suppose it wouldn't hurt doing it again so you can be learning what's what 'bout dusting. I expect you know how dusting goes, but I'll keep an eye on you all the same."

That said, after parading across the room to primp before one of the mirrors, she then plopped herself down on a rich, red-brocaded wing chair, and began at once to give her full attention to her fingernails. Jenny, meanwhile, was left to learn what was what about dusting on her own.

She had not been at work long, and was cautiously lifting a delicate porcelain vase from a table in order to dust around it, when she suddenly heard footsteps coming heavily down the stairs into the entry hall. A moment later, as she looked into the mirror reflecting the wide doorway, she saw Winston Graymark with Jingle at his side go limping past it.

"Blast it, you imp, where did you put my driving gloves?" Winston Graymark growled.

"Right here in my hand, Mr. Winston," came the cheerful reply.

"Oh, all right then," said Winston Graymark gruffly. "But I hope you remembered that I won't be riding Blackguard in today. I'm taking the cart."

"I told Sampson," said Jingle. "If Blackguard's out front and not the cart, it ain't my doing, Mr. Winston."

"Who'll be pulling the cart, then? Is Rocket's leg well enough to—"

The front door opened and closed, cutting off the sound of voices and the rest of Winston Graymark's question. Jenny turned away from the mirror to look out the window, where she saw him descending the portico steps with Jingle. In front of the portico stood a handsome road cart hitched to a sleek chestnut horse, its reins held by a bent, gray-haired man who appeared to be at least as old as Crimpit.

After holding a short conversation with the old man, during which the chestnut's leg was examined and approved, Winston Graymark, with the help of Jingle's shoulder, hoisted himself up onto the cart. He picked up the reins, paused a moment as if thinking something over, and then nodded to Jingle. His face lighting up with a huge grin, Jingle proceeded to jump into the cart and settle himself beside the cart's owner. They then started off at a brisk clip, going faster and faster as they rode down the driveway.

"Rate he goes, one of these days he'll of broke his neck," calmly observed Lilly, who had interrupted her nail work to peer out the window next to her chair. "Almost as bad when he goes flying off on that Blackguard of his. 'Course then he ain't risking anyone else's neck like in the cart. And there's Sampson looking on with nary a twitch on his face. Still, what's to be expected of someone older than Christmas, like half of everyone else around here? Anyway, no business of mine, and soon to be less when I'm wed."

Jenny waited a respectful few moments to see if the wedding subject was to be pursued, but when, surprisingly, it was not, she asked, "Where do they go in the cart?"

Lilly produced a bored yawn. "Oh, just inside the city, down by the docks. It's where Mr. Graymark's business is, which he's took over as head after the old gent got his stroke. Family business from way back, Ma says, where all the money's from. What Jingle does with hisself all day, your guess is as good as mine." She paused to give the room a brief inspection. "Well, looks good enough to me, so now we can go do the library. That's how I arranges my dusting, anyways. You can do whichever way you like. Makes no never mind to me after I leave to be wed."

The library was a room Jenny did not care if she ever saw again in her life, considering what had happened to her there.

"This room takes more care than the rest," Lilly informed Jenny, to her great dismay. She wanted to be in and out of there in the very shortest order. She was so nervous as she dusted that she very nearly knocked over a half-filled wine decanter on a table near Winston Graymark's leather chair.

"Good thing that didn't go over," said Lilly helpfully. "You'd get skinned alive by Mr. Crimpit. Likes his little glass of wine every night, Mr. Graymark does, and only Mr. Crimpit's allowed to fill that bottle from the wine cellar. Well, good thing he's got something else to do besides wait on Mr. Graymark at table and answer the doorbell when he manages to hear it. Most of the time he just sleeps in his rocker in his room. Oh, well, what's it to me, anymore?"

At last, dusting "lessons" in the library came to an end. Her tin bucket filled with rags and brushes, Jenny trudged up the broad staircase with Lilly. When they arrived at the top, it was instantly clear to her why Madame Dupray had referred to the upstairs hall as a "gallery."

There, shrouded in shadows and in deadly silence, rows of brass oil lamps flickered over walls lined with paintings. These were not paintings of storm-tossed oceans like those that loomed over the downstairs rooms, but instead were portraits. Portraits of young women, dowagers in rich silk dresses, pale young men, and old men with long, gray beards. Their fixed eyes stared into the gallery from unsmiling faces, all rigidly imprisoned in carved gilt frames. They were, in truth, as grim as the paintings of oceans that hung on the walls below them.

"Spooky, ain't they?" said Lilly under her breath, as if the portraits on the walls were actually listening. "You see that spot up there? The spot what looks as if another picture might of hung there?"

Awed and not a little frightened, Jenny nodded.

"Well," said Lilly, "my idea is that it was of someone who had an actual smile on their face, so it got took down. The rest of them sour old horrors is ghosts of dead people here to haunt the place. They make my flesh creep, and that's the living truth. Anyways, they might as well know I'm to be wed, so they can't haunt *me* anymore!" She looked defiantly up at the portraits and stuck her tongue out at them.

But then she withdrew it immediately. "Oops!" she muttered. "I shouldn't of done that considering I ain't left yet." Then she rushed through an open door, to all intents and purposes leaving Jenny to fend for herself against the wrath of the ghosts. Jenny, however, quickly followed her through the door.

"All right, this is *his* room," Lilly said. "You might of guessed."

If Jenny had any question as to the "his" referred to by Lilly, it was soon answered by the row of riding boots, one pair still mud spattered, lined up against the wall. Other than that, when compared to the other rooms all so luxuriously furnished, how could any have guessed that this room belonged to the master of Graymark House? Every piece of furniture in it was simple, plain, and well worn, from the chest, to the bed, to the old wardrobe with its scratched and dented doors. In the corner of the room sagged a black, leather armchair, and in another corner, by the window, sat a large, ugly table. On the table were scattered paintbrushes and tubes of paint, the only bright spots in the room. Caught unawares by the sight of the table, Jenny drew back, staring at it.

"That's right," said Lilly. "If you didn't already figure it out, *he's* the one painted all of them ocean pictures. Like I said, spooky's not half the word for it." To impress this point on Jenny, Lilly paused to give a shudder. "Glad I'm to be wed and won't have to see them anymore. Anyways, don't touch them precious paints for your life.

Nor them boots, either. Jingle does them. One of the only things he does, I might like to add. But now I'll show you how to do the bed before you dust and sweep."

The bed made, Lilly retired to the leather chair to observe Jenny learning what was what about dusting yet another room. Then once again she found herself clanking down the gallery with Lilly.

"Madam's room," announced Lilly as they entered yet another door. "More like it, if you ask me."

The room was indeed more like it! Jenny was startled when she saw it, but then remembered that, having to be near her charge, Madame Dupray would no doubt have to occupy a room once belonging to a member of the Graymark family. She might well be a servant, as she said, but this room was a far cry from the servants' rooms in the cellar, as occupied by Jenny and Violet, or even from the room they had just left. In truth, this room was as richly and handsomely furnished as any in Graymark House.

Heavy maroon velvet drapes held back by gold tassels hung at the tall windows. A matching spread lay on the carved mahogany bed. A chest, dressing table, and two chairs were all of gleaming mahogany. But, again, there was one curious furnishing that caught Jenny's attention at once: a wooden trunk sitting between the chairs in front of the windows.

A crocheted white lace coverlet lay over the trunk like a drift of snow, but it did nothing to disguise the fact that the trunk was battered from hard use, its nails and fittings, and even the wood itself from which it was made, blackened with age. It was hardly a piece of furniture in keeping with the rest in the room. But the sight of it made Jenny's heart skip a beat. Was it part of Madame Dupray's past that had caused her to "have great sympathy" for Jenny's situation? Oh, it must be, just like Jenny's own trunk that had come with her from China! She felt curiously drawn to it, and started toward it.

"Where did you think you were going?" Lilly asked sharply.

"To . . . to start my dusting," stammered Jenny, taken aback by the tone of Lilly's voice.

"Not *that* article, you don't," said Lilly. "I did once and got my head snapped off. Madam don't want anything touched in this room . . . not that trunk, leastways, nor any of them pretty silver things stretched out on her dressing table. And she knows if anything's been moved a quarter inch. She does up her own bed, and all you're to do is dust the windows, and sweep the floor and carpet. Peculiar, is all I can say."

To Jenny it did not seem peculiar at all, for she guessed at once Madame Dupray's reasons for giving this order. The Crimpits! Had Madame Dupray not warned her to keep her silver dragon box well hidden lest the Crimpits come searching her room, just as Madame Dupray suspected her own was searched? If anything was disturbed in her room, how was she to know who had done it if someone came in to dust? So Jenny began diligently dusting the windows, convinced she knew something Lilly clearly did not.

As they left Madame Dupray's room, Lilly gave Jenny a knowing, raised-eyebrow look. "Room you do next right beside this one is the old gent's room," she whispered. "Madam or Violet's always there. If they ain't, you don't go in. You just dust around a bit, and pick up the laundry sack. Come to think on it, I'll do the room today. You just follow me round. Madam lets you know if anything else is wanted."

By the time these whispered instructions had ended, they had reached the room in question. Although the door stood open, Lilly still knocked, waiting until she heard Madame Dupray speak.

"You may enter, Lilly, and Jenny may accompany you."

In another richly furnished bedroom, this one much larger than the rest, Madame Dupray sat in a green damask wing chair to one side of the front window. Across from her in a matching chair sat Violet. An open sewing basket with embroidery thread spilling from it lay on a dainty cherry wood table set between them. Both were at work on needlepoint they held on their laps. They barely looked up as Violet and Jenny entered.

Of course Madame Dupray and Violet were not the only ones in the room. In a dark green velveteen armchair at the foot of a tall, four-poster mahogany bed was the stooped figure of a white-haired old man, a gray wool shawl wrapped around his shoulders. He never so much as turned his head to watch Violet and Jenny enter his room, but stared ahead with dull, faded blue eyes from under curiously fierce, heavy white eyebrows. It was impossible to tell if he had seen or heard the girls enter, or if he could even see or hear at all.

This, then, was the Mr. Graymark who was to have been so taken with Jenny's curls and winning smiles had he indeed been acknowledged as Jenny's grandfather! Even though she was now nothing to him but a servant, she felt a sudden lump rise in her throat at the sight of him hunched over so pitifully, as lifeless as the chair that held him. He did not even blink as Lilly carefully dusted the furniture around him, Jenny silently in tow.

"There will be nothing extra today, thank you, Lilly," said Madame Dupray, her voice so flat, she might well have been addressing the design on the carpet.

Whatever hope Jenny might have had for a special glance or smile from her quickly faded. Not on her face or even in her voice was there even a hint of a smile. It was as she had said: They must remain strangers.

"Now," announced Lilly as soon as they had left the room, "you get to learn what's what about doing the washrooms and the laundry."

Well, Jenny had already learned what was what about coal, and dust, and dirty dishes. Further, she had learned what was what about Madame Dupray—who would not, or could not, even acknowledge her presence with a smile—sullen Violet, treacherous Mr. and Mrs. Crimpit, Winston Graymark with his twisted grin, and his toady, Jingle. And finally she had learned about a man too old and feeble even to see or hear her, much less care if he did. Among all of them there was as little comfort to be found as in the grim faces that hung on the gallery walls. Ghosts of dead people! That's what Lilly said they were, and she was right.

Now Jenny was to learn what was what about doing washrooms and dirty laundry. And left to wonder what other lessons still remained hiding in the shadows of Graymark House, lying in wait for her!

Chapter IX

Jingle

A number of dreary days had passed and now Lilly had given notice, and was gone. For the first time, Jenny was doing all the household chores alone. She had never thought she might miss Lilly, her "lessons," and her never-ending reminders of how she was to be wed. But, oh, how Jenny would have liked Lilly by her side as she crept alone past the fierce lion's head up the broad stairs. Facing the angry oceans in the paintings below had been bad enough, but now she must make her lonely way down the gallery with the fixed eyes of the portraits glaring balefully down on her. Were they ghosts, as Lilly had said? They must be, or why else would Jenny feel a cold draft that made her skin prickle as she hurried by them? Their eyes seemed to accuse her of being an intruder, of being someone who had pretended to be Jenny Graymark instead of a mere Jenny Bekins.

Glad to escape into her first room, she found she was not much better off there, for it was Winston Graymark's room. The empty riding boots lined up against the wall only brought to mind their owner and the twisted smile he had had on his face when he had looked at her.

In Madame Dupray's room, she accidentally brushed against the white lace coverlet on the trunk. With trembling hands, she tried to set it back exactly as it had been, for what if Madame

Dupray snapped *her* head off as she had done with Lilly?

But worse of all was when she had to dust the room where Madame Dupray, Violet, and old Mr. Graymark sat in dead silence. By the time Jenny made the journey from that room down the gallery, her heart was drumming so hard in her chest, she could barely breathe. As dreadful as it was, the cold, dank laundry room actually seemed like a safe haven from the rest of the house.

What felt to Jenny like hours later, she was still in the laundry room. But the laundry piles yet to be done seemed to be growing larger instead of smaller. Lilly actually had helped with the wash, seeing that Jenny, at half her size, would never be able to finish it on her own. But it must have proved difficult, just as Lilly had said, to find a replacement among the village girls. So Jenny was alone in the laundry room with nothing to keep her company but the sounds of the waves crashing on the cliff below Graymark House, and the water sloshing in her iron tub.

Her legs soon ached from standing so long on the cold brick floor. Her hands were swollen from the combined effects of the harsh laundry soap and from being sunk in water for so long. Her knuckles were rubbed raw from the fierce crimps of the zinc washboard eating into them. At last, overcome with fright, loneliness, and despair, she could bear it no longer. Throwing her face into her water-soaked hands, she began to sob.

"All right, you can quit your blubbering," a voice beside her growled. "I got sent here to help."

Startled, Jenny raised her face from her hands to find herself looking at the scowling face of Jingle. His cool blue eyes looked back at her with disgust from under the sandy hair falling unkempt over his forehead.

Eyes still brimming with tears, Jenny was unable to do anything but stare at him.

"Here," said Jingle, dipping into a pocket of his baggy, faded gray shirt and pulling something out. "Take it and wipe yourself up."

He handed Jenny what was little better than a filthy rag. Further, when she wiped her eyes and nose with it, it gave off a very strong smell of horse.

"Th-Thank you," said Jenny with another sob as she handed Jingle back his rag.

"Keep it," he said roughly. "But don't start in blubbering again. It ain't pleasant for me. And you might as well know I don't like being here no more'n you do. Doing laundry ain't what I was handed an invitation for. But it 'pears like I don't got no more choices'n what you do. Don't do like we're told, you get shipped back to China, if that's where you really come from. And I get shipped back to Pa, who ships me off to the factories."

All the while Jingle was talking, he was rolling up his sleeves. "Now," he said, "let's get on with this creeping laundry. I ain't aiming to spend the rest of my creeping life here."

His skinny arms began pumping fiercely up and down a washboard like the pistons of a steam engine. Up and down. Up and down. And all the while his lips were tightly compressed, his face stony. It was clear that all conversation with Jenny had ended except what was necessary to say regarding passing the soap, or asking where the clothespins might be hidden. In less than half the time it would have taken Jenny alone, the laundry was hanging on lines stretched across the room, and Jingle was rolling down his sleeves.

"I'm outta here," he said, starting for the door. Then he hesitated and turned around. "Maybe I will take back my handkerchee."

Jenny had strongly considered throwing it in the trash bin, but had politely stuffed it into her pocket. "Thank you again," she said stiffly, and handed it back to him.

Jingle just shrugged. "I might need it, and with any creeping luck, I ain't coming back." With that, he wheeled around abruptly and fled the room as if he had a pack of wolves at his heels.

So, if Jingle had any luck, he would not be back. Well, Jenny thought, if *she* had any luck, he would not be back. But then she softened. After all, he *had* lent her his "handkerchee," such as it was. And think how much help he had been! How would she ever have finished her washing without him?

On the other hand, Jenny remembered, he had only helped her because he had been forced to do so. And had he not taken back his precious "handkerchee"? No, he was a horrid boy, and fit companion only for the likes of such as Winston Graymark.

But standing there thinking about all this did nothing toward getting her work done, Jenny soon concluded. Besides, further thinking might only end up bringing more tears, and she had no time for that. She still had all the ironing to do from yesterday's laundry, and even some from the day before. And what a murderous task ironing was! First heating the heavy irons on the oil burner, then struggling with them to the ironing board, and finally running them over the linens. Up and back. Up and back, with the irons feeling heavier and heavier all the while. Irons were not called "sad irons" for nothing, thought Jenny, for ironing must surely be the saddest job in the world.

Before beginning her ironing, however, she must run up to the kitchen, where Mrs. Crimpit would have left her something for her noon meal. And Mrs. Crimpit would have left something else as well—all the dirty dishes from everyone else's noon meal. But before going to the kitchen, there was something else Jenny needed to do. With all the sloshing and splashing of water, especially on the part of Jingle, her dress was soaking wet. It had by now become dingy and stained, with tears on the sleeves and the hem of the skirt. It was altogether disreputable looking, but Jenny had not had the courage to change to another dress since this was the one chosen by Madame Dupray. Now she determined she must hang the dress up to dry, at least for a while. And she must find something else to wear.

Her small wooden trunk had appeared in her room soon after

her arrival. She had looked inside it but had taken nothing out, as there were no nails left on the wall to hang anything. Further, the few dresses held by the very small trunk were, she was sure, no more suitable than others. But perhaps she had overlooked one she could wear just while her other was drying. So she ran down the hall to her room and, kneeling on the floor, she opened the lid of the trunk. And drew in her breath sharply at what she saw.

Somebody had been going through her things in the trunk! They were not in higgledy-piggledy disarray, but there was no question in Jenny's mind that somebody had been there. Her dresses were not folded as she remembered them, but it appeared that someone had tried to make them look as if they were. Who could it have been? And why would they have done this?

And then once again Jenny remembered Madame Dupray's warning. The Crimpits! One of them, probably Mrs. Crimpit, had come snooping in Jenny's room. Where else besides the trunk might she have looked? Swiftly, Jenny ran to her cot and lifted the mattress.

Her little silver dragon box was there, but in not quite the same place as she had left it. Again, someone had tried to make it look as if it had not been touched. Who had done this? And when? She had not opened the trunk or looked at her dragon box in many days.

Could it really have been Mrs. Crimpit, the little old lady with the dim smile? And then Jenny thought of old Mr. Crimpit, whose eyes had grown so hard when he had begun to suspect she was not who she said she was. Could not Mrs. Crimpit's eyes grow just as hard behind her tiny spectacles? Oh, Jenny would have to be very careful around the two of them, just as Madame Dupray had warned. Very careful indeed!

Chapter X

A Forbidden Visit

ꟷ

The following day, as Jenny was dusting the parlor, she looked out the window and saw the same scene being enacted that she had viewed with Lilly a number of days earlier. It was that of Winston Graymark's cart careering down the driveway, carrying not only its owner, but Jingle as well. So it seemed that he had indeed been lucky, and had escaped having to help with the laundry again.

Well, that must mean Jenny was lucky, too, and someone had been found, after all, to help her. She was ready to welcome anyone who would not only help with the work but would keep her company as well. And if that anyone might be young, it could be someone who would prove to be her friend. Intent on this daydream, she never heard the soft footsteps that came up to the door and stopped.

"Jenny?"

She spun around to see a tall, black apparition that had suddenly materialized at the door. It was Madame Dupray standing there in a black hat and coat as stern and stark as the dress she without doubt wore under it. Over her arm hung a large, ugly black leather satchel. As her eyes fastened on Jenny, she stood pulling black leather gloves over her long, pale fingers.

"Y-Yes," stammered Jenny.

"This is my day off, Jenny," Madame Dupray said. "I will be away until late afternoon. Violet, of course, will act in my place. So anything she asks of you, you must do. Is that clear?"

"Oh, yes!" Jenny replied, and offered a trembling smile.

If a smile was returned, it was so slight, and so stiff, it could well be called no smile at all.

"Very well," said Madame Dupray. She pulled her watch from her satchel and snapped open the lid. "I must hurry," she muttered, shaking her head and frowning. "The coach will be here at any moment."

When she had left the house, Jenny watched her walking quickly down the long driveway that Jenny herself knew to be treacherous with its ruts, slippery fallen leaves, and sharp gravel. Surely the Graymark wealth could provide a carriage to take Madame Dupray to her destination, Jenny felt. But then she remembered what Madame Dupray had said. She was only a servant like Jenny. And servants must take the public coach, no matter how far one had to go to catch it.

Knowing of Madame Dupray's departure, Jenny was not surprised to find only Violet in the room with old Mr. Graymark when she arrived to dust his room. Although Violet gave her the same forced smile she always did whenever their paths crossed, today she seemed particularly stiff and uncomfortable. In truth, she kept her eyes lowered the whole time Jenny was there dusting.

"There will be nothing extra today," she said when Jenny was preparing to leave. But she said it with her eyes fastened on her embroidery, seeming to avoid in every possible way looking into Jenny's own eyes.

Jenny had hoped that Violet might be more friendly toward her when Lilly had left. But she believed now that would never happen. Her only hope lay in someone else coming to Graymark House, perhaps that very day! Perhaps even there already! She decided to go find out right away, leaving one washroom to do after her midday meal. She rushed down the stairs to the laundry room.

But no one was there. Nor any sign that anyone had been there. Or was even coming. Jenny was all alone with the same tubs, the same washboards, and the same cold sad irons. Jingle must have weaseled his way out of the work, and into Winston Graymark's sympathy, assuming he had any.

Oh, that miserable wretch of a boy, and his filthy "hand-kerchee"! Jenny, who had actually had little prior knowledge of boys other than the boys in broad, white collars and velvet knee britches who were brought to the dance studio by their mothers, could only wonder about this one. Her disappointment at not having a new helper all but disappeared in her rage over this—this *boy!*

But Jenny had no time to stand about being angry. For while this wretched *boy* was dashing about the countryside in a grand cart and having a fine time in the city, she had work to do, and no one to help her. And she still had to go back upstairs to do another washroom, left undone needlessly, as it turned out. So with laundry and the midday dishes done, she went wearily trudging back up the stairs.

She had still not grown used to the gallery. Nor could she forget what Lilly had said of the paintings. Ghosts of dead people! All glaring at her as she crept by them! Today, the gallery seemed particularly gloomy and foreboding, and she was especially glad to escape into the washroom. There she began at once to scrub the basin, humming a small tune remembered from dance studio days to keep up her flagging spirits.

Then, all at once, over the sound of her humming, she heard a blood-chilling sound, the sound of a terrible moan. Though Jenny had not entirely believed what Lilly had said, she believed it now! The moan could only have come from the gallery, from the ghosts that haunted it! As she stood frozen in the washroom, her heart pounding, the ghastly sound came again. She knew she must escape. But, how? How would she dare make it past those frightening eyes to the safety of the staircase?

And then she realized that Violet and old Mr. Graymark were in a room far closer to where she was than the stairway. Never mind what Violet would think if she came bursting into the room. That is where she had to go. Running from the washroom, not looking to right or left, she fled down the gallery. Without even stopping to knock, she burst unceremoniously into Mr. Graymark's room.

She was just in time to hear him calling out the words, "Water! I would like a cup of water, please, Violet."

That was the "moaning" Jenny had heard! Filled as it was with Lilly's observations, her mind had played tricks on her! And now she must explain away to Violet what she had just done. But where *was* Violet? She was nowhere to be seen!

Why was Violet not at Mr. Graymark's side with a cup of water? Why was she not even at her usual place by the window with her embroidery in her lap? No longer terrified by the imagined moans, Jenny now had something else to fear. After all, she had had strict instructions not to be in that room unless Madame Dupray or Violet was there. And here stood Jenny in the room, with old Mr. Graymark calling for water, and no Violet in sight.

"M–Mr. Graymark, p–p–please don't be afraid," she said in a quavering voice. "Violet is only gone for a moment. She will be right back. I shall go fetch her at once."

Certain that Violet had only gone to visit the other washroom, Jenny went there at once, only to find the washroom empty. Next, no longer thinking of the portraits, Jenny sped down the gallery. Violet must be found, and at once! Perhaps she had gone to the kitchen to fetch a pot of tea, or even to her room in the cellar. But neither of those places produced any sign of Violet.

Jenny knew that old Mr. Graymark was not to be left alone for very long, so she hurried back to his room. She only hoped that wherever Violet had gone, she would now be back in the room. But when Jenny arrived, there was still no Violet.

"Oh, Mr. Graymark," Jenny said, "Violet will be back soon. I know she will. But I will fetch you your cup of water."

Filling a cup from the jug that sat on the chest, she gave it to him and waited until he had taken a few sips.

"I am always so thirsty when I first awaken from my afternoon nap," he said, handing her back the cup. "Thank you, Jenny. That is your name, Jenny, isn't it?"

"Yes," replied Jenny, nodding.

"What a pretty name . . . Jenny," Mr. Graymark said. "Now, won't you stay and visit with me awhile? Perhaps you might read me a few pages from my favorite book. It is *Oliver Twist,* by Mr. Charles Dickens, and it is over there on that small bookcase. Have you been taught to read, child?"

"Oh, yes!" said Jenny eagerly. "But . . . but I can't do it! I musn't!"

"May I ask why not? And why do you look so frightened?" asked Mr. Graymark, his white eyebrows drawn together in a puzzled frown. "Are you afraid to be reading to an old man?"

"Oh, no, no, no!" cried Jenny. "But I'm not supposed to be in this room unless Madame Dupray or Violet is here as well. I *did* look for Violet everywhere, indeed I did, even in her room. But I could not find her, and what am I to say if Violet returns and finds me here?"

"Why, only the truth, Jenny," replied Mr. Graymark. "You were cleaning nearby, and heard my cry for water when I awoke from my afternoon nap. That is all there is to it. And now will you fetch the book?"

Although still frightened, Jenny could not refuse old Mr. Graymark's request, so she went to the bookcase. Moments later, she was perched on the four-poster bed, legs dangling over the side, and opening the red leather book to the red ribbon marking the place where the last reader had left off.

"'Oliver Twist, Chapter Twenty-three,'" she read. "'The night was bitter cold. The snow lay on the ground, frozen into a hard thick crust, so that only the heaps that had drifted into by-ways and corners were affected by the sharp wind that howled abroad: . . .'"

Instantly lost in the story, Jenny forgot all her fears as she read, until four pages into the chapter she heard the *thump-thump* of footsteps running down the gallery toward the room. Quickly she slid from the bed, but did not have time to return the book to the bookcase, so stood there book in hand when Violet came flying into the room, her hair in disarray and her cheeks flushed.

"Why . . . why are you here, Jenny?" she asked, so breathless, she could barely speak.

"I . . . I . . . I was cleaning nearby when I heard Mr. Graymark call for water," said Jenny, also hardly able to speak, but for quite another reason: Her heart had jumped into her throat from fright.

"Well . . .well . . .well," stumbled Violet, clearly trying to collect her thoughts. "I . . . I was only gone for a moment to . . . to my room to . . . to fetch something."

Needless to say, all three people in the room knew that Violet was lying. She, also needless to say, was not going to say so. Nor, indeed, was Jenny. But what would old Mr. Graymark say to it? Nothing, as it turned out. He simply stared at Violet without even blinking.

"But what are you doing with that book, Jenny?" Violet asked suddenly, taking attention away from herself.

Jenny's throat now felt as if it had closed up completely. Why had old Mr. Graymark not told her what she was to say about the book? She swallowed hard, and then swallowed again. "I . . . I . . . have it because . . . because," she finally blurted. But not another word could she utter.

"Why, she has it because I asked her to fetch it," Mr. Graymark interrupted calmly. "I wished you to read to me when you returned, Violet."

"Oh!" said Violet, which was really all there was left to remark on the subject. "Well, you may give me the book and then leave, Jenny."

Thrusting the book into Violet's outstretched hand, Jenny fled the room. She ran and she ran, and never stopped running until she reached her cellar room and threw herself facedown on her iron cot, knowing new fears had been added to the ones she already had.

Would Violet tattle on her to Madame Dupray? That would mean, of course, that she would have to confess that she had left her post with old Mr. Graymark. But could she not simply lie again? After all, surely she would be allowed to go to her room "to fetch something," as she claimed to have done.

And what of old Mr. Graymark? He had not appeared the least disturbed by Jenny's presence in his room without Madame Dupray or Violet, as Madame Dupray had said he would be. But old as he was, could he be trusted to say nothing about it?

And as for Jenny herself, what could she do about any of it? Nothing! And all of this because she had wanted to go looking for someone in the laundry room—*anyone* in the laundry room who might prove to be a friend.

Chapter XI

Friendly Overtures

𝕋

𝕋he next day, when Jenny went to do her dusting chore in old Mr. Graymark's room, it was as if nothing unusual had happened there the day before. Madame Dupray and Violet sat by the window silently doing their embroidery. Old Mr. Graymark sat huddled in his chair, his faded eyes staring ahead with no expression in them. Well, *almost* no expression. For did she not detect the same spark in his eyes she thought she had seen the day before? And for Jenny, it meant he intended to keep the secret! As for Violet, it appeared that she was not going to risk punishment for her own part in what had happened by tattling on Jenny.

So the secret was safe for the moment, and a great weight was lifted from Jenny's mind. But she had learned a lesson. When she had been instructed not to do something, she would not do it. No matter what! So when she heard the front doorbell ring as she was descending the stairs into the downstairs hall, there was no question about Jenny's answering it. After all, Lilly had informed her that it was Crimpit's job to answer the doorbell. "And no one else!" warned Lilly.

In truth, Jenny did not think she should even *be* in the hall— with her hair in shreds, her dress torn, her hands full of rags, mop, and a bucket—as someone was welcomed into the front door of Graymark House. Since she expected Crimpit to arrive at once, she knew she could not escape the hall in time. So she dropped down on the top step just where the stairwell curved around, and sat safely hidden by the stair railings. There she waited. And waited. But Crimpit failed to appear.

The bell rang again, and still there was no sign of Crimpit. It rang a third time, a long, hard, angry ring. Jenny now came perilously close to running to the door, never mind the warning from Lilly. But just as she was on the dangerous point of jumping up from the step, Crimpit finally came shuffling from the dining room into the hall. As soon as he opened the front door, a man, very tall and very narrow, in a black woolen cloak and broad-brimmed hat, carrying a large black leather case, came striding into the hall.

"Where were you, Crimpit?" the man said in an annoyed voice. "I had to ring *three* times." Setting down his case, he peeled off his cape and hat and thrust them unceremoniously at Crimpit. "Dozing off, I'll wager. I keep telling Mr. Graymark that he ought ... oh, never mind. Well, I've come to pay my respects to Mr. Graymark Sr. I trust he is in his room, and that Madame Dupray is with him?"

"I believe so, Mr. Slorkin," replied Crimpit, clearly allowing nothing to ruffle his butler's feathers as he hung up the cloak and hat on the hall coatrack. "I shall go up at once and announce your arrival."

"No, no, you'll do no such thing, Crimpit," said Mr. Slorkin impatiently. "I don't intend to wait here for you to make your torturous way up and back. I have been inconvenienced enough by having to wait at the door. I know where to go, of course, and will announce my presence myself." He started for the stairs, and then, perhaps having second thoughts about his rudeness, paused. "But thank you all the same, Crimpit."

Jenny, in the meantime, had grown more and more horrified by this man's rude behavior toward Crimpit. Crimpit might well be as crafty as Madame Dupray had said, but he was still an old man and should not be spoken to in that manner. And then suddenly Jenny realized with equal horror that this dreadful man must pass right by her on his way up the stairs! If he spoke in such a manner to Crimpit, what would he have to say to a ragged little cleaning girl who was not only in his way but who had been eavesdropping as well?

As it turned out, she had nothing to fear on that score. For one terrible moment, he did pause to stare at her. She found herself looking up into a long, narrow, colorless face, all of whose features—long, pinched nose, sharp, pointed chin, and thin, bloodless lips—were perfectly complemented by the pair of hooded eyes no less chilling than those of a cobra. But they looked down on Jenny as if she were of no more importance than a filthy rag in her bucket, and then he went on his way, moving silently and deliberately up the stairs like a dark specter.

It was as well that Crimpit was so slow in leaving the hall, because for a few minutes Jenny was too paralyzed by this encounter to move. But as soon as his footsteps could no longer be heard, she jumped up from the step. Fast as her legs and the mop and the rattling bucket she carried would allow, she raced to the cellar, arriving breathless in the laundry room. But it appeared that someone had arrived there ahead of her. It was Jingle, already standing at a washtub, rolling up his sleeves.

"Well, I'm back," he said with a careless shrug. "Where you been? Why you looking like you just swallowed something you wasn't expecting?"

Well, why would Jenny not look like that, if "surprised" was what Jingle meant? After all, she had never expected to see him again in the laundry room. "I've been dusting and cleaning upstairs like I always do," replied Jenny primly. Since she was offended at the questions, she chose only to answer the first one. What right had this—this *boy* to ask her questions, anyway?

But Jingle either did not notice her stiff tone, or else chose to pay no attention to it. "I dust and clean, too . . . in the stable," he said, as if they had just been holding any ordinary conversation. "Mostly clean, I guess, 'cause that's what you do with horses. I do some grooming, too," he added proudly. "Sampson says I ain't bad at it."

He hesitated for a moment, and then abruptly pulled something from his pocket. It looked suspiciously like the same dirty rag he had handed Jenny two days earlier, which in truth it was.

"Here," he said, "take it back. I know it ain't very clean. You can put it in the wash if you like."

Suspicious of the change in Jingle's behavior, Jenny put out a wary hand to take the rag. "Thank you," she said uncomfortably.

"I shouldn't of took it back from you once I gave it to you," Jingle said. "That's what Mr. Winston told me."

"M–M–Mr. Winston?" faltered Jenny. "Do you mean Mr. Winston Graymark?"

"The one!" replied Jingle. "Told him I found you blubbering when I come to help with the laundry, like I got told to do. Said to him I'd give you the handkerchee, but took it back. He gave me what for 'bout that. He tries to learn me creeping manners, and what I done weren't mannerly, he said. Trying to make me speak proper, too, so I can be a better valley to him. But that ain't going to be easy."

Jenny had now heard enough of Winston Graymark's ideas about Jingle's manners and speaking properly, not to mention Jingle's future as his "valley." Was this not the same dreadful man who had condemned Jenny to life as a servant, where all that mattered was dusting, and scrubbing, and mopping, and dirty laundry? What did any of that have to do with manners and speaking properly?

She drew herself up as far as her eleven-year-old self would allow. "I don't wish to hear any more about Mr. Winston Graymark," she said in a well-starched voice.

Jingle, who had already started scrubbing, stopped to fix a

stern look on Jenny. "Look," he said, "Mr. Winston ain't so bad. And it ain't his fault you ain't who you said."

"Well, it isn't *my* fault, either!" Jenny flung back.

"So somebody done you a bad turn," said Jingle, beginning to scrub again. "That's the creeping party what ought to get the blame."

None of this had changed Jenny's feelings one bit about Winston Graymark. Of course, even though only at the request of Madame Dupray, he had *not* shipped her back to China. On the other hand, had he not, by allowing her to stay, found a free servant for Graymark House just, as it turned out, when one was needed? Yet had he not then seen to it that Jingle came to help her? Back and forth bounced these thoughts in Jenny's head as she scrubbed on in silence. And in the end, was not what Jingle said true? The "party" really to get the blame was the one who had done Jenny the "bad turn." But who was that "party"? Who? And *why?*

For some minutes there were no sounds in the cellar room but the sloshing of water in the tubs, and linens being rubbed on the crimps of the washboards. At long last, Jingle gave Jenny a sideways look. "You really come from China?" he asked.

Jenny nodded.

Jingle thought a minute further. "Do they really eat with them little sticks over there?" he asked.

Jenny stifled a giggle. "They're called chopsticks," she said, in truth feeling rather superior at knowing this.

"Did *you* eat with 'em?" asked Jingle.

"Sometimes," replied Jenny. "When we ate Chinese food, we did."

More thoughtful silence from Jingle. "Could you show me how?"

"I don't expect we can find any chopsticks," Jenny said. But when she saw the crestfallen look on Jingle's face and realized that this was a serious request, she quickly added, "But perhaps we can find some sticks that will do just as well."

Jingle produced a satisfied grin as he returned to his scrubbing. After a few more minutes spent in thought, he turned again to Jenny. "What was it your pa, whichever one you called your pa, anyways, did in China?"

"He had a dance studio with Mama," Jenny replied, and immediately wished she had thought to lie or pretend not to have heard the question when she saw the disbelieving look Jingle gave her.

"Dance studio?" He thought this over, but then only shrugged. "That how come you was wearing that dress with all them rosebuds and ribbons when you first got here?"

"Yes," replied Jenny simply.

"My sister would of liked that dress," Jingle said.

"Do you have sisters?" asked Jenny.

"A bunch," replied Jingle glumly. "But . . . but she's the one I don't have anymore."

"Oh!" said Jenny. "I . . . I'm sorry."

"Ain't your fault," Jingle said, and fell silent again.

"What does *your* papa do?" Jenny asked finally.

"He delivers coal," replied Jingle. "It's how I come to be here. Mr. and Mrs. Crimpit knew 'bout me when I helped Pa with the coal. Caught me just in time. Pa was fixing to get my little brother to help him, and I'd be put in a creeping factory. So I got put here instead. I like it here."

"Even if you have to do laundry?" asked Jenny.

"Aw, ain't that bad," said Jingle.

After this, the conversation flagged. But when they were hanging the linens on the lines to dry, Jingle said suddenly, "You like dogs?"

"I don't know," replied Jenny.

Jingle's eyebrows flew up. "What does that mean, you don't know? Ain't you never seen a dog?"

"Yes, but not up close," said Jenny, remembering the mangy,

starving mongrels with their ribs poking out that roamed the streets where she had lived in China, and which she had not been allowed to go near for her life.

Jingle shook his head in disbelief. Then he gave a big sigh. "Look, you get to eddicate me 'bout them . . . them *chop*sticks, now I get to eddicate you 'bout something. Looks like we finished up here early, so you got plenty of time 'fore you got to be in the kitchen. I got something to show you in the stable."

Jenny suddenly had the terrible feeling that Jingle was going to present for her approval some fearful cur that she would actually be supposed to touch and exclaim over. But it came to her that, unlikely as it seemed, she might almost be starting a friendship with—with—with this *boy*. It was only a beginning friendship, however, and might be shattered by the smallest of missteps. So with a fainting heart, as soon as the laundry had all been hung up, Jenny meekly followed Jingle from the laundry room and down the dimly lit cellar passageway.

Chapter XII

A Surprise in the Stable

⚜

To Jenny's surprise, Jingle passed right by the cellar steps that led to the kitchen.

"Aren't we going to the stable?" she asked, still not quite trusting anything Jingle might do.

"It's what I said, ain't it?" he replied.

"But how can we go outside if we don't go through the kitchen?" Jenny asked.

Jingle stopped in his tracks. "You mean you didn't know there's steps down this end going straight out?"

Jenny shook her head.

"Well, now you know," he said matter-of-factly, and continued on his way with Jenny scurrying after. "It's the steps what bring me when I come down to the laundry room. Same steps that Sampson and Digger, he's the one what takes care of the outside, and sometimes me, take when we come to put coal in the furnace."

By now they had arrived at a steep stairway and were halfway up its old, crumbling brick steps when Jingle looked over his shoulder at Jenny. "You mean you go all round by the kitchen anytime you go outside?"

"I haven't gone outside," replied Jenny. "Not since I've come here."

"Wheeoo!" Jingle gave a low whistle before continuing up the steps. "Then you got a treat coming," he said as he reached the top and pushed on an old door, which creaked painfully on its rusted hinges as it swung open. "You get to see the ocean from outside. Ain't it something?"

Jingle seemed to have forgotten that Jenny had not so long ago seen a great deal of ocean. It was not the same one, to be sure, but was an ocean all the same, and she had spent days and days crossing it. But after the confines of the gloomy house, and her dismal cellar room, the fresh, sharp smell of salt water, and the sight of a sun, just breaking through the mist and sparkling on the water, was, just as Jingle had said, "something."

"You got to be careful of the cliff, 'cause it's crumbly," Jingle said. "Mr. Winston's always warning me. But when you got the time, you can come on out and go up to the edge out there and see it closer. We can't stand round now, howsumever, 'cause I still got something to show you in the stable."

Jenny had hoped that Jingle might have forgotten the "something" in the stable, for she still envisioned a mangy cur that she was expected to admire and, worse still, actually pet. But on Jingle marched, across a wide, graveled space, past a wooden building that held the Graymark House carriages, and at last into the stable where Jenny was greeted by the pleasant smell of hay, and by horses with their soft, gentle eyes looking out at her from their stalls. How much she would have enjoyed this if only that "something" did not lie ahead that Jingle was so determined to show her!

"Brung Jenny to see something, Sampson," Jingle announced as they passed the old man at work polishing a saddle.

He looked up and gave Jenny a broad smile that made no attempt to hide the spaces where five teeth were missing. "Ain't unhappy to make your acquaintance, Miss Jenny. But best try not to wake anybody up, Jingle. They only just et and went down," he said, aware, it appeared, of the "something" Jenny was doomed to see.

But Jenny had caught the word "they." Were there more than

one that she must contend with? On Jingle went all through the
stable to the very farthest corner. At last he stopped and beckoned
to Jenny. Hesitantly, she crept over. What she saw crunched up in
the corner was a shabby, well-worn quilt of no definable color, a
quilt that must have seen service in the stable for as long as old
Sampson had been there. On the quilt lay a large, butterscotch-
colored dog surrounded by three butterscotch-colored and two
black puppies not three weeks old. The puppies were all sound
asleep, but the mother dog was awake, watching Jingle and Jenny
approach.

Jingle's arm shot out, holding Jenny back. "We got to see how
Polly takes to the notion of us getting close to her babies," he
whispered.

They waited a few moments, barely breathing, and then the
dog's tail began a slow *thump-thump-thump* on the ground.

"It's all right," Jingle said. "We just got permission to come see
the babies." He motioned to Jenny to come closer to them. "Well,
what do you think?"

Jenny was almost too overcome to speak. "Oh, Jingle!" she
cried softly.

"Ain't they worth bringing you out for?" he asked.

"Oh, yes!" said Jenny. "May I touch one?"

"Just do it gentle," Jingle replied. "Like Sampson said, they
oughtn't to be woken up just yet."

Jenny knelt down beside the quilt and, reaching out a hand,
lightly touched the head of one little sleeping butterscotch-
colored puppy. It felt warm and soft as velvet. All the puppies with
their tiny ears and tails and special puppy smell were like an
enchantment. Jenny felt she could stay kneeling there forever.

"Oh, Jingle," she whispered, "they are . . . they are truly magi-
cal!"

"That they are!" he said.

"Do they have names?" Jenny asked.

"Not yet. Mr. Winston and Sampson and . . . and *me,*" he added proudly, thus making certain Jenny knew he was part of the naming committee, "ain't got round to it yet, but one puppy ain't no doubt to be Sailor, on account of that was Mr. Winston's dog, which was these puppies' grandpa. *All* the puppies come all the way down from one what was once old Mr. Graymark's dog. Her name was Janey."

Once old Mr. Graymark's dog!

"Jingle," Jenny said excitedly, "wouldn't it be nice to call one of these puppies Janey, too, and . . . and perhaps take it in for Mr. Graymark to pet? He looks so sad all the time, and I know it would cheer him up. I believe he'd far rather have a visit from a puppy than that terrible man who came to pay his respects."

"What terrible man is that?" asked Jingle.

"His name is Mr. Slorkin. I was just coming downstairs from my cleaning chores when Mr. Crimpit let him in," Jenny explained. "But he is a very rude and ugly man. I don't see how anyone like that would cheer up Mr. Graymark."

"You ain't far off the mark 'bout him being rude and ugly," said Jingle. "That's Mr. Obadiah Slorkin. He's what they call general manager of the Graymark Shipping Company. I don't much like him, and near as I can tell, he ain't got much use for me. I think he got other ideas for a valley for Mr. Winston, but lucky for me, Mr. Winston got his own ideas, like keeping on old Mr. and Mrs. Crimpit, and Sampson, and Digger."

"But what about the puppy?" Jenny asked. "Could we take one up to Mr. Graymark?"

"Don't see how," said Jingle, frowning. "Madam and that sourpuss Violet ain't going to allow it. And one of them's always hanging round up there like creeping black spiders. From what Mr. Winston says, when Madam gets her day off, sourpuss Violet is there. When she gets her half day, Madam is there. I don't know personal 'cause I never been allowed in the old man's room. I ain't never even met him. But that's what Mr. Winston says, anyways."

Jenny had to bite her tongue, for it was all she could do not to blurt out how Madame Dupray and Violet *had* both been gone at the same time. But she was not ready to trust Jingle with a secret in which she was a culprit as well as Violet. What if Jingle should, even if by accident, report it to Winston Graymark? Besides, Jenny still had no idea where Violet had gone that day, or even if she would ever go there again. Telling Jingle was not worth the risk. "Well, then," she said, "may *I* come to see the puppies again?"

"No problem with that," replied Jingle. "Only best you don't come 'less I come with you, 'cause Polly ain't been round you much. And tomorrow I can't come."

"Oh!" said Jenny. It was a very disappointed "oh."

"But see here," said Jingle quickly. "What I got to do tomorrow is run an errand for Mrs. Crimpit in the village. Only got to buy her some thread and a paper of pins, so won't take but an hour. You can come with me, if you like. We can go early afternoon. Maybe when we get back, we can come see the puppies."

"But what about my ironing?" asked Jenny.

"Aw, don't worry 'bout that," said Jingle carelessly. "The ironing ain't going noplace. It'll still be here when you get back."

Which was not exactly what Jenny wanted to hear. But then she had no reason to expect Jingle to help with the ironing as well as the washing. Besides, he did have his own work to do. But he had invited her to go with him on a trip to the village, and perhaps later to come visit these beautiful puppies again. And had he not introduced her to them in the first place? Oh, yes, at that moment, Jenny was willing to forgive him anything, even if the ironing *doubled* before she got back!

The next afternoon, just as Jingle had promised, he and Jenny went trudging down the road on their way to the village. They had left by way of the cellar stairs, and no one had seen them leave.

Still, Jenny was not at all certain she should be on this venture. After all, Jingle had been asked to go, but she had not.

"Do you think it's all right for me to be leaving the house?" she asked anxiously. "Nobody ever said I could."

"Anybody ever said as how you couldn't?" asked Jingle. "Anybody ever said as how you was in prison?"

"N-No," replied Jenny.

"Well, then," said Jingle, and no more was said about it.

"Do you go often with Mr. Graymark to the city?" Jenny asked, remembering that this was the very road on which they traveled.

"How did you know 'bout that?" Jingle asked.

"I see you leave when I dust the parlor," replied Jenny. "And you said you knew Mr. Slorkin, who is at Mr. Graymark's company."

Jingle grinned. "Ain't you the clever one, figgering all that. But I don't go often as I'd like."

"What is it you do when you're there?" asked Jenny.

"Just wander 'bout," replied Jingle. "Sometimes Mr. Winston takes me down to see one of the ships. Other times I go see Ma. Mr. Winston gives me a bit of money to take to her. She don't get many nice things. Pa takes all the money Mr. Winston gives for me."

"Oh," said Jenny, who had now learned one more reason why Jingle must have such a different view of Winston Graymark than she did!

But they soon reached the cluster of cottages and small shops that made up the village. One shop bore the sign JONES'S DRY GOODS over the door, and that was the door Jingle entered. While he was making his purchase of pins and thread, Jenny wandered about, marveling at how one little store could hold so many different and exciting things. On one shelf she even saw two beautiful dolls with real hair. Curls! Just like the ones she had had shorn from her head. She could not take her eyes from the dolls.

"You ain't pining away for them curls, are you?" asked Jingle, having finished with his purchase and come up beside her. "If you wish to know the truth, you look better without 'em, even if you didn't get the best chopping job from Madam, if she's the one what done it. Besides, you got to remember, you ain't a doll, so your hair's going to grow out." Jingle, clearly a disciple of Winston Graymark, then muttered under his breath, "Creeping curls, too, more's the pity!"

Looking at the dolls with a supreme air of indifference, he started for the door, but then suddenly stopped, grabbed Jenny's arm, and pulled her back. "Uh-oh! Look out there!" He pointed out the shop window. "Who'd of thought you'd see *that* picture?"

Across the street, cozily arm in arm, were a pair of young women, and a more unlikely combination of two people could hardly be imagined.

One was distinguished by a flat, ruddy face topped by a grand, incredibly large balloon of bright orange curls, the whole lot rising up from the collar of a moth-eaten rabbit-fur jacket. From the latter descended a long skirt of white and brilliant pink stripes so weighted down with pink bows, and so narrow, that its owner, hampered additionally by high-heeled boots that she was plainly unused to wearing, could only move with the tiniest of precarious, mincing steps.

The second young woman, her pretty face capped by dark hair severely drawn back in a knot, wore only a somber black dress and coat, with no ornaments or ribbons to be seen.

The two were, of course, Lilly and Violet, strolling down the street, smiling, chatting, and gazing into shop windows.

"Forgot it's Violet's half day," Jingle whispered, as if they could actually hear him. "We'd best wait until they pass on. I know you ain't been told you can't leave the house, but no sense in taking chances."

"So that's where Violet must have gone," Jenny murmured to herself.

"Gone where? When?" asked Jingle, quick to pick this up.

"I . . . I . . . I . . . ," Jenny stammered, and then clamped her lips shut.

"See here," said Jingle. "You can't 'I . . . I . . . I . .' and that's all there is and there ain't no more. You've gone and let the cat out of the bag, and 'lest you know a good way to get it back in, you'd best finish what you started."

Jingle was right, Jenny knew. She now had to tell him every-thing. So as soon as Lilly and Violet had disappeared, and she and Jingle were on their way back to the house, she told him the whole story of all that had happened on Madame Dupray's day off, from the moment Jenny had first thought she heard ghosts moaning in the gallery.

"Wheeoo!" whistled Jingle. "Don't blame you for being spooked by them creatures on the wall. But they ain't got voices, and looks like there's nobody else is going to tell on you to Madam. I know *I* ain't, for certain. Anyways, it 'pears to me as how you learned something from all what happened."

"I know," said Jenny. "It's that I must never again do what I've been told not to do, no matter what."

"Not what I had in mind," said Jingle. "I say what you learned is that there might be another time when *both* them creeping spi-ders leave their web. And what that means is—"

Jenny interrupted him with a gasp. "I know! It means that we can take the puppy for old Mr. Graymark to see!"

Jingle nodded, with the pleased look on his face of a cat who has just caught himself a mouse.

"But what if Violet never does that again, go off to visit Lilly while old Mr. Graymark is taking his afternoon nap?" Jenny said.

Jingle's eyes narrowed. "Oh, I expect she'll go again. I expect she'll go every chance she gets. Never seen her with much but a look on her face would sour milk. And there she was with an actual smile on her face. What do you think of that?"

Well, Jenny had seen an actual smile on Violet's face before, but it was one forced from her by Madame Dupray. At any rate, Jenny had no interest in discussing Violet's smiles, or lack of them. All she was interested in talking about, and even thinking about, was the journey to old Mr. Graymark's room accompanied by Jingle—and a puppy named Janey.

Chapter XIII

Secret Messages

ᛟ

Slowly. Carefully. One tiptoed step at a time. Jenny and Jingle crept up the staircase. In Jingle's arms, wrapped in his treasured old horse blanket from the mattress in the stable loft that served as his bed, was a precious butterscotch-colored puppy, now soundly asleep.

Only the *ticktocking* of the clock in the library broke the deep hush that hung over Graymark House. Mr. and Mrs. Crimpit were at their afternoon naps in their quarters. Madame Dupray was away on her day off. And Violet? Well, Jingle, posted where he could observe the comings and goings from the house, had seen her come flying out shortly after the time of old Mr. Graymark's scheduled nap.

"Just as I said," Jingle reported to Jenny with a self-satisfied grin.

"But what if Mr. Graymark is still asleep when we get there?" Jenny asked anxiously.

"Well, it's like we already agreed," said Jingle. "We'll wait long as we can. If he never wakes up, we got to wait till another time. 'Course then the puppies will be older, and won't be so easy. We'll just have to wait and see."

Now they were about to do just that, for they had arrived at old Mr. Graymark's room. And it was just as Jenny had feared. He was in his chair with his head drooping on his chest, to all intents and purposes as sound asleep as the puppy in Jingle's arms. Jingle looked at Jenny, shrugged, and shook his head. Should they wait awhile, as they had agreed? But how long could they really wait before it became too dangerous to wait longer?

Then, suddenly, old Mr. Graymark gave a start. His head snapped up, his eyes opened, and he was staring at Jenny, smiling. "I was hoping you might return, child," he said.

"Did we awaken you?" Jenny asked with a worried frown. "Oh, I hope we did not!"

"Oh, no, no, no," said Mr. Graymark. "I was only dozing. But I shall let you in on a secret. I had pretended to be asleep so Violet could escape. It isn't right for a young woman to be imprisoned with the care of an old man for so many days on end as she is. But I'm not such an old man that I couldn't put two and two together after what happened last week. And I know how long I'm supposed to be napping, so I will simply pretend to be waking up when she returns. But I see you have brought a friend with you, Jenny."

"Oh, yes!" said the delighted Jenny. "This is Jingle. He is Mr. Winston Graymark's . . . his . . . his . . . *valley.*"

"His 'valley,' eh?" said old Mr. Graymark, a twinkle appearing in his eyes. "I've heard about you, I believe, and am glad to make your acquaintance, Jingle."

"P-P-Pleased to make yours, too, s-s-sir," Jingle said, plainly quite overcome by this event.

"We've brought something to show you, Mr. Graymark," said Jenny shyly. "Jingle, show Mr. Graymark."

Jingle slowly approached the old man, laid the bundle in his lap, and carefully unfolded it. For moments, Mr. Graymark said not a word, simply sitting and gazing at the puppy. At last, he raised his hand and, with one finger, gently stroked its head. "Oh, children! Oh, children!" These words and the look in his faded old eyes were all that was needed to let Jingle and Jenny know how much what they had done meant to him. "Does the puppy have a name?" he asked.

"It's to be Janey, sir," replied Jingle.

"Why, that was *my* dog's name!" exclaimed Mr. Graymark.

"I know," said Jingle. "It's what Sampson told me. He says Polly, their ma, and all the puppies come down from your Janey. Anyways, it's what we want to call this one, if Mr. Winston ain't against it. We all get a say in it, sir . . . Sampson, Mr. Winston . . . and," again he added proudly, *"me."*

Mr. Graymark shook his head. "Don't be too disappointed, Jingle, if the puppy won't be Janey after all. You see, Mr. Winston doesn't always try to . . . well . . ." He gave Jingle a reassuring smile without finishing what he was about to say. "Never mind, she's Janey for now!" He continued petting the still sleeping puppy for a few moments, but then looked anxiously up at the clock on the wall across from him.

"Oh, Violet is not due back yet, Mr. Graymark," Jenny quickly reassured him.

"I know," he said. "But, Jenny, I must tell you that my reason for hoping that you would be back today wasn't only that I wished you to read to me again as you did so very nicely the last time. I'd like you to do something else for me. Could you hurry to the library and find in the desk there a tablet of paper, a pot of ink, and a pen, and bring them back to me?"

"Oh, yes, if you wish it, Mr. Graymark," replied Jenny, anxious to do anything to please him.

"Go as quickly as you can, child," he said. "There is something I must write before Violet or . . . or anyone else returns."

Leaving Jingle behind with the puppy, Jenny did not waste another moment before running from the room. The portraits were nothing more than a blur as she flew down the gallery, then down the stairs to the library. There she quickly found all that old Mr. Graymark required. Back in his room, she knelt by his side holding the ink for him while he, with pen in hand and tablet of paper on his lap, began to write.

At first he started to speak the words as he wrote them. "I, Winston Christopher Graymark III, being of sound mind, if not of sound body, do hereby . . ." But then he began to murmur the words so they were no longer intelligible.

All the while he wrote, he cast quick glances up at the clock, racing against time. On and on his pen scratched, but at last he was finished. Folding one sheet of paper, he wrote on it the name CRIMPIT, and handed it to Jenny. Then he carefully folded together the remaining several sheets of paper on which he had written and, with his old hands shaking from his efforts, handed them to her as well.

"Can I trust you, Jenny, to see that these are delivered to Crimpit as quickly as possible?" he asked.

"Yes, Mr. Graymark," Jenny replied. "Oh, yes!"

"And please remember that no one but Crimpit is to know about this. Can I trust you, Jingle, as well as Jenny, not to betray me?" Mr. Graymark gave Jingle a long, searching look.

The wide-eyed Jingle nodded his head so hard, it seemed he was trying to shake it right off his shoulders.

"Now go, children, go!" said old Mr. Graymark. "It is almost time for Violet to return. You must hurry. And I thank you for all you have done for me!"

Jenny, bearing the secret letters entrusted to her care, as well as the paper, pen, and ink to be returned to the library, and Jingle with the puppy bundled in his arms, waved to old Mr. Graymark, and then ran from the room.

But they were no more than halfway down the gallery when they heard footsteps running up the stairs. Jenny suddenly felt the puppy somehow thrust into her arms and herself pushed in an open door.

"Duck down behind the bed!" commanded Jingle.

As Jenny ducked, she saw Jingle picking up a pair of mud-spattered boots that sat just inside the door. For indeed, they were in Winston Graymark's room! As Jingle stood in the doorway, diligently examining the boots, Violet went flying by, a panic-stricken look on her face.

"Afternoon, Violet," said Jingle cheerily as he calmly flicked a bit of dried mud off one boot.

But it was a solemn, thoughtful Jingle who came down the stairs with Jenny as soon as Violet had disappeared. Yet who could wonder at this? He had heard old Mr. Graymark start to say something about his son, Winston, that might lead someone to think there was something amiss between them. Then Jingle had been witness to old Mr. Graymark writing secret letters, letters so secret that only those in the room and Crimpit could know of them.

It seemed that the afternoon had produced more than just an adventure with a puppy. Oh, yes, a great deal more!

Chapter XIV

A Theft in the Library

ҭ

I t was after the dishes from the midday meal had been cleared
away that Jenny went tiptoeing into the library. In truth, there
was no real need to tiptoe. It was one week following the adventure with the puppy, and Madame Dupray was once again away on
her day off. Mr. and Mrs. Crimpit had disappeared into their quarters for their naps. Whether old Mr. Graymark was napping or not,
Jenny did not know. But what she did know was that Violet was
with him.

She believed Violet had been so startled and frightened at seeing Jingle standing in the doorway of Winston Graymark's room
that she would never again desert her post to go visiting Lilly in
the village unless it was her proper half day off. She had no way of
knowing, of course, that Jingle would not have reported her crime
to Madame Dupray for his life. But there was every reason to
believe she would not risk it again.

It saddened Jenny to think they might never again be able to
take the puppy up to old Mr. Graymark, although on that day they
could not have done it anyway, even if Violet were not there. For
Jenny had seen Winston Graymark beckon Jingle into the cart that
morning and ride off with him. So Jenny had no help with the
laundry, and no visit to see the puppies, either. She had thought to
take her first walk along the cliff at last, but the day had suddenly

become cloudy. So she decided to visit the library instead.

Ever since she had read to old Mr. Graymark, Jenny had been longing to have a book to read when she was alone in her room. The library had dozens—no, more like hundreds—of books lining its walls. Surely one would not be missed if she were to help herself to it. She would not be stealing it, after all, but only borrowing it. Still, her mission had not been approved by anyone, and she could not help feeling guilty as she tiptoed in.

Soon, however, she was lost in the joys of pulling one book after another from the shelves, carefully putting each one back before pulling out another. Though many of the books appeared dry and dull, many looked interesting enough that she was certain she would find just the right one.

How long she had been there she had no idea, for she had lost all track of time when, over the steady *ticktocking* of the clock, she heard the creak of wood on the staircase. This was followed by another creak, and yet another, coming closer. Footsteps were coming down the stairs, taking someone where? To the dining room? To the parlor? To the front door? Was Violet escaping after all? The footsteps quietly crossed the hall—to the library!

Jenny dropped to her knees like a stone behind the chair nearest to the bookshelves. Thoughts raced dizzily through her head. Although Crimpit's old legs almost never took him up the stairs, what if it *was* Crimpit coming into the library, as he often did, to fill the wine decanter and see if all else was in order for Winston Graymark? And what if he was to find Jenny crouching guiltily behind the chair? Would it not be better if she stood up quickly and pretended she had returned to finish dusting the room? But before jumping up, Jenny peeked cautiously around the edge of the chair. And found it was not Crimpit who had entered the library. It was Violet!

She was creeping stealthily toward Winston Graymark's chair by the fireplace. When she reached the table beside the chair, she stopped. Jenny could only see her back, but it was certain from the way her arms were moving that she must be doing something with her hands. Then Jenny heard the sound of glass rubbing against glass, as if the stopper of the decanter were being pulled out. Beyond that, she could not tell what Violet was doing. But Jenny could make a very good guess. Violet was helping herself to a drink from Winston Graymark's wine decanter!

Jenny was struck numb with disbelief. What on earth did Violet think she was doing? Jenny, herself on a guilty mission to the library, was after all only borrowing something. Violet was *stealing!* Furthermore, Violet was drinking something Madame Dupray could not possibly approve of for a young woman not yet twenty, and a servant at that. But what could Jenny do about this?

Nothing? Of all the choices that later went drumming through her head, that was the one she most preferred. But if she did tell someone about Violet, whom would she tell? Mr. and Mrs. Crimpit would surely see to it that Violet was dismissed from Graymark House. Winston Graymark would dismiss her himself, though Jenny would be terrified to face him with what she knew. He might even simply give her his twisted grin and not even believe her. After all, had she not represented herself as Jenny Graymark when it seemed she was no such thing? And if you could tell a tale about one thing, could you not tell a tale about another?

Yet if he or Mr. and Mrs. Crimpit did believe her, would Jenny want Violet dismissed? It was true that she was not overly friendly to Jenny, but then she had done nothing to harm her. And Jenny did not wish to do anything to harm Violet. Oh, if only she could talk this over with Jingle. But she could not. Jingle already had one secret he must keep from his Mr. Winston, so how could Jenny ask him to keep another? And a secret, for the time being, it must remain.

But Jenny really knew that in the end, she had to tell some-one, someone who could talk to Violet. And the someone, Jenny realized at last, must be Madame Dupray! Of course, she had told

Jenny that if anything must be said to her, it must be through Violet. Well, this was a case where Jenny had no choice but to speak to Madame Dupray directly, and without Violet present. Violet's half day was four days away, so that meant Jenny must wait, and in the meantime, tell no one.

The next morning, Jingle came thumping into the laundry room at high speed, his eyes wide with excitement. He had his own news, which he was quite willing and able to share with Jenny. "Guess what, Jenny? Mr. Winston and me, we almost got kilt!"

"How?" cried Jenny. "What happened?"

"Had to do with the cart," replied Jingle. "You ain't going to believe this."

Yes, remembering what Lilly had said about the way Winston Graymark drove his cart, Jenny could very well believe this. "Rate he goes, one of these days he'll of broke his neck," Lilly had said.

"Well, what *did* happen?" asked Jenny, suspecting she already knew the answer.

"It were this way," said Jingle, having to catch his breath before going on. "Just before Mr. Winston and me was getting ready to come home, he was standing by the cart talking with one of the clerks. Happened to look down, and good thing is all I can say. Two, maybe three, maybe even four wheel spokes been messed with. Almost sawed right through. Mr. Winston said if we'd hit a rut, we'd gone right over, and good-bye to our necks. Broke in two, more'n likely."

"Who could have done such a thing?" exclaimed the horrified Jenny. This was certainly not what she had expected to hear.

"Mr. Winston thinks it's somebody playing pranks," said Jingle.

"It wasn't a very nice prank," Jenny said indignantly.

"No, it weren't," agreed Jingle. Then, surprisingly, he grinned. "But got something else to tell you. Whilst I were wandering 'bout town, not going no place in partiklar, guess who I seen?"

Jenny dutifully shook her head.

"Well, who I seen weren't who I thought," he said. "But gave me a start, 'cause I thought I seen Madam parading down the street. She stopped in front of this sweetshop, and who should come up to meet her but Mr. Obadiah Slorkin! In the two went, and up went I to the window to peek in."

"Oh!" gasped Jenny.

"Turns up it weren't Madam after all," said Jingle with a rueful grin. "This lady's face were all painted up like Christmas, with these big shiny earrings dangling from her ears most to her shoulders. Her hair were all done up in these creeping big sausages, and her dress . . . wheeoo!" Jingle stopped to whistle. "You never seen the likes. It were 'bout the same as that dress you was wearing the night you come here . . . begging your pardon, Jenny . . . all covered with posies and ribbons. Enough to put your eyes out!"

"Did they see you?" asked Jenny. "What would Mr. Slorkin have done if he'd caught you spying?" Jenny shuddered, remembering her encounter with Mr. Slorkin on the stairs, and the look he had given her as he passed by her.

"No fear," Jingle replied. "I was mighty careful, you can bet on that. Anyways, I didn't stick round long, and the whole time Mr. Slorkin and this lady had their eyes glued one to the other. I ran back, and it were 'bout then Mr. Winston found out 'bout the wheel. Whilst we was standing round waiting for the wheel to be changed by the man from the carriage shop, I got round to telling Mr. Winston 'bout Mr. Slorkin and the lady. Well, Mr. Winston just throws his head back and laughs fit to bust, and he ain't one who laughs much, neither. 'Why, that sly old dog!' says he. 'You won't say nothing to him 'bout it, will you?' says I, not wishing it known I were the one what was doing the spying and passing the tale along. 'Never you fear,' said Mr. Winston. 'Your part in this discovery will remain locked with me.' But can you guess what he said next, Jenny?"

Jenny shook her head, for how could she possibly imagine

what would come after both these astonishing events?

"Why, he just said he wondered if that weren't Madam's *sister,* on account of my saying how at first I thought it were Madam I seen on the street. Then he goes on to tell me how it were Mr. Slorkin who knew 'bout some rich people's housekeeper in the city, which was Madam, just when Mr. Winston needed somebody to look after his pa. He said Mr. Slorkin told him 'bout a sister Madam don't have much use for, but Mr. Winston had forgot all 'bout it. Seems to me," concluded Jingle, "it's how Mr. Slorkin knew of Madam, 'cause her sister's his lady friend!"

It seemed so to Jenny as well, and was it possible that this sister, the exact opposite of Madame Dupray, might even have something to do with the mysterious past that made her plead Jenny's case with Winston Graymark?

What Jingle had to relate that morning almost made Jenny's discovery in the library pale by comparison. Yet she still wanted to talk to him about it. If only she could! But her mind was made up about it. There was one person she could confide in: Madame Dupray. The *only* one!

Chapter XV

A Good and Kind Child

⚜

Violet's half day arrived, and immediately after Jenny finished her noon kitchen duties, she started on her journey back upstairs. Today the eyes of the gallery portraits seemed to bore holes right through her as she crept past them. This time not because she was an intruder, but because she was about to be a shameful telltale! But she did not falter, because she knew she must do what she had determined to do.

Arriving at old Mr. Graymark's room, she drew a deep breath and then knocked at the door as she always did. As it was old Mr. Graymark's nap time, Madame Dupray did not call out, but instead rose and came quickly to the door. "Yes? What is it, Jenny? Did you forget something?"

"N-No," said Jenny. "B-But I must speak to you, Madame Dupray."

"Then let us step into the gallery to do so," said Madame Dupray. "We must not disturb Mr. Graymark. But, Jenny," she said sternly, "do you not remember what I told you, that any messages you have for me must be delivered through Violet?"

"Oh, yes, I *do* remember," said Jenny. "But this is something . . . oh, you must believe me, Madame Dupray . . . I could not speak to Violet about."

Madame Dupray frowned. "Is . . . is it something about Mr. and

Mrs. Crimpit, Jenny? They are nice old people, my child, but even nice old people can be crafty, as I warned you. Did . . . did they search your room, as I suggested they might? And did they find your precious little silver dragon box?"

Jenny nodded. "I believe they did. But they didn't take anything," she hastened to add.

"I am relieved, indeed, to hear that," said Madame Dupray with a gentle sigh. "Yet if not that, then what is it you needed to speak to me about?"

"Madame Dupray, it is about Violet herself!" Jenny blurted.

"Violet?" Madame Dupray's eyes flew open. "What can you possibly have to tell me of Violet?"

"Oh, Madame Dupray, it is about something I saw Violet do. I . . . I had returned to the library to . . . to finish my dusting," Jenny said, praying that her face would not betray this terrible lie, "when Violet entered the room. I was behind a chair in the room, and she did not see me. I would have spoken to her," Jenny said, guiltily lying again, for it was only Mr. Crimpit she would have spoken to, "but, oh, Madame Dupray, Violet was so quick in what she was doing, and when I came to realize what it was, I felt I had turned to stone, and couldn't speak."

Madame Dupray blanched. "My child, you frighten me. What is it you came to realize that she was doing?"

"Madame Dupray, she . . . she was stealing a . . . a drink from Mr. Winston Graymark's wine decanter!" Jenny burst out.

"Did you actually see her doing this, Jenny?" asked Madame Dupray.

"N-N-No," Jenny faltered. "I only saw her from behind. But I heard her open the decanter, and it was easy to guess what she was doing."

Madame Dupray was silent for a few moments, her eyes thoughtful. "Jenny, I believe you are quite right in what you suspected. But have you told anyone else of this?"

"No! No!" Jenny cried. "I've told no one but you, Madame Dupray. But I knew I must tell someone, for what if Violet were to do it again?"

"You are quite right to have reported it, Jenny, and to have reported it only to me," said Madame Dupray. "If word of this were to reach the ears of Mr. and Mrs. Crimpit, or Mr. Winston Graymark, Violet would surely be dismissed."

"I was afraid she might," said Jenny.

"Well, you are a good and kind child," said Madame Dupray. "It would be cruel if Violet were to lose this position. She sends most of her wages to her needy family. You may be sure I will speak to her at once. I do not believe she will do this again, but if you find out that she does, you will report to me at once, will you not, Jenny?"

"Oh, yes!" said Jenny, at last able to breathe normally again. How right she had been in determining to make this report! And how very, very right she had been in choosing to make it to Madame Dupray!

Madame Dupray had somehow managed to wipe away every one of Jenny's feelings of guilt. So for the first time since she had discovered Violet's stealthy visit to the library, Jenny climbed into her cot at night with a conscience clear and light as a bubble, and was able to drop off to sleep almost at once.

Tap! Tap! Tap!

Something woke Jenny, and she opened her eyes sleepily, staring into the dark cellar room. Then she closed her eyes again, preparing to go back to sleep.

Tap! Tap! Tap!

Now Jenny's eyes flew wide open.

Tap! Tap! Tap!

Thoroughly awake now, she realized that someone was at her door. Her heart began to beat more quickly. Who could be calling

on her in what must surely be the middle of the night? Was it
Madame Dupray again?

Jenny scrambled from her cot and ran across the room. She
opened the door a crack. Then she opened it further, and drew in
her breath sharply. For standing before her, lantern in hand, wearing only her long nightdress, was Violet!

"May I come in, Jenny?" she asked. The small flame in her
lantern danced about wildly as the hand that held it trembled.

Jenny stepped back so Violet could enter the room.

"I *am* sorry to be coming here so late and waking you," Violet said, giving Jenny a wan smile. "But I could not sleep for wishing to come to thank you."

"Th-Th-Thank me?" said Jenny, stumbling. "Wh-Wh-What-
ever for?"

"Why, for not reporting what you saw me doing in the library
to anyone but Madame Dupray," Violet replied.

Jenny froze, words caught in her throat. She had never
dreamed that Madame Dupray would not only "speak" to Violet
about what she had done but would go so far as to tell her who
had spied on her in the library and reported her!

"Aren't you very angry with me?" Jenny asked, her voice
shaking.

"No," said Violet. "For you only did what you thought was
proper. And you thought to tell only Madame Dupray. If you had
told . . . told anyone else, I would have lost my position here. And
I cannot lose it. I must not!" Violet paused, wringing her hands.
"So do you understand why I cannot be angry with you, Jenny?
And if you wish my forgiveness, I give it willingly and gladly."

"Thank you!" said Jenny earnestly. "Oh, I do wish it, indeed!"

Violet hesitated. "But perhaps I should ask your forgiveness,
Jenny," she said. "I know I've not been as kind to you as I might.
I am several years older than you, but that is no reason for us not
to be friends. Perhaps tomorrow afternoon, if Madame Dupray

will excuse me and you can take a little time off from your chores, we might go strolling by the ocean. I think it's so beautiful out by the cliff. Do you go there often, Jenny?"

"I have never been at all!" exclaimed Jenny. "But I've wanted to."

"Then perhaps you can go there for the first time with me," said Violet. "And you can tell me something about your home in China, for Madame Dupray has told me that is where you are from. And if you would, you can tell me how it feels to cross a wide ocean, and not just look at it from the cliff. Would you do that?"

"Oh, yes!" said the delighted Jenny.

After Violet left her room, Jenny had difficulty in believing that Violet had even been there, and all that had happened as a result. For now Jenny not only had Jingle as a friend, but might have Violet for one as well. And all because she had gone to the library to find a book!

Chapter XVI

A Terrifying Encounter

𝕿

"Jenny," said Mrs. Crimpit the next morning, "Mr. Crimpit's come down with a little touch of the flu, so would you take Master Win's breakfast tray in to him? There's a dear. I think you can manage it."

Mrs. Crimpit was, of course, as wrong as she could be, because Jenny's legs were suddenly preparing to buckle right under her. Ever since the night in the library when she had first arrived, she had managed to escape being anyplace near Winston Graymark. Busy with kitchen work, she never entered the dining room until he had left. She was generally dusting in the parlor when he left for the city in his cart, with or without Jingle. And she well knew the sound he made when he walked. *Thump. Drag. Thump. Drag.* Whenever she heard that sound approaching, whether he was leaving the house to ride horseback, or was accompanied by Jingle carrying the easel and canvases, Jenny managed to duck through any open door near her. Now she was being asked to serve him his breakfast in the dining room!

As she waited with legs about to collapse, Jenny hoped against hope that Mrs. Crimpit would offer to carry in the tray herself, or that Jingle would magically appear from the stable and take it in. But neither happened, and so *Jenny* went, clutching the tray and going slowly and cautiously into the dining room. Her hands were

trembling so violently, the dishes danced about on the tray, clink-
ing and rattling noisily. Worse, the coffee in the coffee cup went
sloshing right over the rim into the saucer!

Winston Graymark was reading a letter from a small stack
lying beside his place setting on the table. Deep in his letter, he
gave no sign of hearing Jenny enter, even with the dishes rattling
as they were. But when she set the tray down on the table, he
looked up suddenly. Scowling when he saw the tray, he slammed
down the letter in his hand. "Oh, take the confounded tray back!
I don't want any of it!" he growled. Then he grabbed his forehead
and pressed hard on it. "Blast this headache! Blast everything! I
don't know why I even came in here this morning. Blast! Blast!
Blast! I feel terrible!"

With that, he pushed himself furiously away from the table,
snatched up the stack of letters, and went stumping from the
room. Jenny stood motionless watching him go, her stomach a
cold, hard knot. Was the sight of her so painful that he had to go
storming from the room with a headache, and without touching
his breakfast? It was all she could do not to burst into tears as she
carried the tray back to the kitchen. Would Mrs. Crimpit be cross
with her as well?

But when Jenny arrived back in the kitchen, Mrs. Crimpit
simply looked at the untouched tray and gave a deep sigh. "Hardly
touched yesterday," she said. "Not touched at all today."

"He . . . he said he had a headache," Jenny said apologetically.

"That's all right, Jenny," said Mrs. Crimpit. "He had one yesterday as well. It must of gone worse on him. He must go see Dr.
Penwick, and so I shall tell him."

Jenny was almost in tears again, but this time from relief. Mrs.
Crimpit had not only not scolded her but had even smiled at her!
Jenny knew Madame Dupray to be right, that Mrs. Crimpit—as
well as Mr. Crimpit—was a long-time servant very much attached
to the Graymark family, and therefore not always to be trusted

where others were concerned. Still, Jenny could not help liking this gentle, old woman. If only she had not gone rifling through Jenny's trunk or snooping until she discovered the precious silver box. And if Jenny only knew why!

"Guess what?" said Jingle, arriving in the laundry room later that morning in a high state of excitement. "Mr. Winston told me someone was at the wheels of his cart again! He says it's someone playing more pranks. But, then again, he says maybe it ain't."

"Oh!" gasped Jenny. "Do you think someone wants him to have an accident in his cart?"

"Ain't you the clever one," said Jingle. "That's exact what he's beginning to think."

"But who could it be?" asked Jenny. "Does he have any idea?"

Jingle rolled his eyes. "Ain't got any clue. He ain't got enemies what he knows of. He keeps to hisself pretty much at work, but he is as fair to everyone what works for him. Ain't a reason for anyone to wish to do him harm."

"Then maybe it *is* just someone playing a prank after all," said Jenny.

"Maybe," said Jingle doubtfully. "But one thing, Jenny, it ain't doing them creeping headaches he's been having last day or two any good. He ain't feeling tip-top, and Sampson ain't pleased 'bout it. Thinks Mr. Winston oughtn't even to go riding."

"He . . . he didn't eat his breakfast this morning," said Jenny.

"How'd you know that?" asked Jingle.

"I had to take it to him because Mr. Crimpit wasn't well," replied Jenny. "Mr. Graymark wasn't very pleasant about it when I brought it in."

"Not pleasant to you?" Jingle asked quickly.

"No," said Jenny. "Just angry about his headache, I think."

"Can't blame him," Jingle said. "Anyways, it don't sound too good, but nothing I can do 'bout it." He paused a moment. "Say, after we done this, we'll go see the puppies. Maybe after that, if we got time, I'll go with you out to see the ocean."

"I . . . I can't," said Jenny uncomfortably.

"Whyever not?" inquired Jingle. "We're getting everything done, ain't we?"

"Because . . . because . . ." Jenny stopped a moment in confusion. "Violet has already asked me to go walking with *her*."

"Violet?" Jingle's eyes looked ready to burst from his head. *"Violet?"*

"Yes," Jenny said, and, feeling a little cross at having to defend this, repeated, "Violet."

"How did that come about?" asked Jingle, eyeing her suspiciously. "What's she all of a sudden want with you?"

"She came to my room last night and . . . and invited me. She . . . she was *very* nice." Jenny, of course, was feeling *very* guilty at not telling Jingle why Violet had come to see her in the first place. But there was no way she could tell him, and that was that.

"Well, too bad 'bout seeing the puppies," said Jingle in a tight voice. "You ain't planning to tell her 'bout them, I trusts?"

"Oh, no!" exclaimed Jenny. "I won't say a word."

"Better not!" grumped Jingle. "Violet!" he muttered under his breath. "Creeping Violet! Hmmmmmmph!"

Jenny, who would much rather have gone with Jingle than with Violet, at this point had no intention of telling him so.

The laundry team continued their work in stony silence. Then the disgruntled Jingle, to further show his displeasure, left Jenny before the laundry was even quite finished. So she was all alone when Violet appeared in the room, already in her coat, to fetch Jenny for their walk. Jenny, who had remembered to bring her own coat with her, was ready in a moment to leave with Violet.

"It is gray out, but the sun may appear at any moment," said Violet. Though she attempted a smile, her voice was dull.

"Oh, I hope so," replied Jenny, trying to sound as if it mattered whether the sun was out or not.

Conversation seemed hard to come by, so they walked in silence down the cellar passageway. But Violet turned off at the stairs to the kitchen, so she must have never learned of the other flight of stairs. And Jenny chose to say nothing about them. After all, those stairs led to the stable, and she did not think she wished to have Jingle see her leave for her walk with Violet.

When they left the house and started down the path to the cliff, Violet acted quite the opposite of the way she had the night before. Her face was set, and she kept her eyes fixed on the path. At last she gave a sigh, as if it was a great effort to speak. "Did . . . did you enjoy living in China?" she asked.

"Yes, because I lived with Mama and Papa," said Jenny, who had no idea how to reply to such a question. Well, after all, she had certainly enjoyed living in China more than she enjoyed where she was living at the moment!

"Oh," Violet said, and fell silent again. It was clear to Jenny that she could have said anything at all and it would have made no difference.

They walked on in silence, Jenny wondering what she could say that would interest Violet. Should she ask if Violet knew anything of Lilly and whether she was wed? Lilly was a subject Violet should be interested in. But before Jenny could decide if it was wise to bring up the subject of Lilly, they had neared the cliff's edge, and Violet herself made another attempt at conversation. "Did you enjoy your trip across the ocean?" she asked.

"Only sometimes," replied Jenny. "Sometimes it was frightening when there was a storm."

"But it is beautiful here, isn't it?" said Violet. She moved away from Jenny, right to the edge of the cliff.

"Oh, you mustn't go so close!" Jenny cried out.

"Whyever not?" asked Violet over her shoulder. "It's perfectly safe if you're very careful. Come along! You mustn't be frightened."

Jenny inched forward. And as she did, Violet stepped backward so she ended up a little behind Jenny. Jenny then turned toward her, and saw that Violet had a hand stretched out before her as if to catch Jenny in case she should stumble. But then she looked at Violet's eyes. They had turned very dark, almost black, and were glaring like headlamps. In truth, they scared Jenny.

Then, abruptly, Violet dropped her hand and gave a piercing cry. "No! No! No!"

She whirled about on her heels and, clutching her long black skirt, went stumbling up the path toward the house.

"No! No! No!" she continued to cry as she fled, a hand to her mouth to stifle her cries.

Jenny watched her in horror. She could not imagine what had happened so suddenly. But then all at once she knew! All that had taken place the night before was an act on Violet's part to lure Jenny to the place where she now stood! Violet actually hated Jenny for spying on her and then reporting it to Madame Dupray. Grateful to Jenny? Oh, lies, lies, lies! In truth, she hated Jenny so much that, although she had lost her nerve at the last moment, she had had every intention not of protecting Jenny at the cliff's edge but of pushing her off it, without any doubt to her doom!

Chapter XVII

A Mysterious Journey

꭛

Jenny decided not to go to Madame Dupray to tell her what had happened with Violet. Not yet, anyway. In truth, Jenny was afraid to go to her a second time, for it might seem that Jenny was now making up stories. Or perhaps Madame Dupray would simply say that Violet was very upset, and Jenny must be more understanding? What then?

Jenny could not even bring herself to tell Jingle about it. In the several days since that afternoon, he had been remarkably silent on the subject of Violet. The walk along the cliff had never been mentioned. Jenny knew he did not like Violet. But murder? Even Jingle might question the story and believe Violet was just being, well, "sourpuss" Violet. And, after all, Jenny had no proof of anything, like a cart wheel that had been tampered with.

She would more than likely be inviting a grin and an "I told you so" where Jingle was concerned. Still, every time Jenny remembered the look in Violet's eyes, she knew she was right. She must, she knew, tell someone of her fears. And soon!

In the meantime, for two nights she had awakened from a terrible nightmare. It was the same both times: a hand reaching out from the darkness and pushing her into a black hole. She would be falling, falling, falling, until she would awake, cold and shivering. Then, on the third night, the nightmare seemed more real than ever. When she awoke, she seemed to feel a hand shaking her shoulder. And there was a voice saying her name. "Jenny! Jenny!" The voice was a hoarse whisper.

Her eyes flew open, and were at first blinded by a lantern held close to her eyes. Then the lantern moved away, and she could see the face of the person holding it. It was Winston Graymark! She gave a cry of fright, and felt a rough hand clamp over her mouth.

"I'm sorry to frighten you," Winston Graymark said. "But you must be silent. I promise you, nothing bad is going to happen to you. If I take my hand away from your mouth, will you promise not to make any sound?"

Almost paralyzed with fear, Jenny was barely able to nod. The hand was removed from her mouth at once.

"Good!" said Winston Graymark. "Now listen to me carefully, Jenny. You may be in danger here, so I'm taking you away to a place where you'll be safe for a day or two until someone comes for you. There's no time now for explanations, but you'll know the reason for this soon enough. For now, just throw your coat over your nightdress and gather up a dress and what few things you might need for one or two days." His eyes darted around the little room. "Ah, I see you have your carpetbag here. Pack it quickly, and we'll be off."

With her teeth chattering, her hands trembling, Jenny some-how managed what she had been asked to do.

"All right, then, come along," Winston Graymark said as soon as she had her carpetbag ready. But as he started for the door, he saw Jenny hesitate. "Well, what is it?" he said. "What's wrong? You know you must come with me, Jenny. And you must come now."

"There . . . there is something I have to take with me," Jenny said.

"Then get it quickly," Winston Graymark said.

Jenny ran to her cot, lifted the thin mattress, and pulled out her silver box. Thrusting it into her coat pocket, she then ran to the door. Winston Graymark made no comment, but simply started silently down the cellar passageway with Jenny at his side. As they passed the closed door to Violet's room, Jenny shuddered. What if Violet should be awake and decide just then to pay her another late-night visit? Violet, who now never raised her eyes when Jenny came to dust old Mr. Graymark's room. But Violet's door remained closed and dark, and from behind it there was not a sound.

They went all the way to the end of the passageway, and then up the crumbling brick steps. From there they moved into a bone-chilling deep fog. A few steps more brought them to the ghostly outlines of the cart and horse, barely revealed by the lantern that hung from the cart. Also revealed was another ghostly outline, which turned out to be Sampson, standing beside the cart with a solemn face, flapping his hands on his arms for warmth.

"All ready, Master Win," Sampson said.

"My thanks, Sampson," said Winston Graymark. "Now, if you'll just lend me your shoulder to get up here."

"Sure you'll be all right t'other end, Master Win?" Sampson asked anxiously. Setting Winston Graymark's lantern on the floor of the cart, he then lent his shoulder as requested.

"I'll manage," Winston Graymark said. "Getting down is never a problem. But would you help Jenny up, please?"

As if she were no more than the weight of a feather, Jenny felt iron-strong arms lift her up and set her down on the seat beside Winston Graymark. It might have been true, as Lilly had said, that Sampson was older than Christmas, but there was nothing very old in the strength of his muscles.

"You drive with care, Master Win," Sampson warned as he set Jenny's carpetbag at her feet. "It's mighty thick out."

"So I've noted. Never fear, Sampson, I'll take care." And it was clear from the outset that Winston Graymark had no intention of driving in the manner Jenny had seen him leave the house before. *Clop! Clop! Clop!* The horse's hooves seemed to be moving at an almost funereal pace as they went down the driveway.

Jenny was by now in a kind of trance. Everything seemed so unreal that she could almost believe she was still asleep. *Clop! Clop! Clop!* As the hooves drummed slowly on through the black night, the lanterns casting a pale, eerie light through the swirling fog, Jenny felt curiously carried back to the night she had arrived at Graymark House.

How much had happened since that time when, frightened but full of hope, she had come with ringlets and a flower-and-ribbon-bedecked dress to her new home! Now she was riding in a cart, transformed into a servant girl, beside a man whose presence she had come to dread. He claimed he was taking her to safety. Why? And from whom? Violet? But how could he know what had happened at the cliff's edge unless from the most unlikely source in the world, Violet herself?

Or could he, like Violet, have invented a reason to draw Jenny away from Graymark House with some deadly purpose in mind? Oh, no, no! *No!* How could this man hunched up beside her be so evil, so wicked as to want to end her life? But, then, had not Violet done just that?

Clop! Clop! Clop! The hooves provided a direful accompaniment to the thoughts twisting and turning in Jenny's head. Turning and twisting. *Clop! Clop! Clop!* Until at last the cart pulled to a stop. But where were they? Darkness surrounded them like a heavy cloak. All Jenny could see were two ghostly lights gleaming at them palely through the fog.

"All right, Jenny, come along with me. And don't forget to bring your bag," said Winston Graymark. Climbing heavily down from the cart, he lifted the lantern from the floor and waited for Jenny to arrive at his side. Then, holding up the lantern, he started up a path toward the two lights.

The small, fluttering light of the lantern barely pierced the dense fog. But it proved enough for Jenny to see that they had come to a tiny cottage with ivy vines curling over an arched door framed by two lighted windows. It was hardly the place her grim thoughts had led her to believe they would come.

A small brass knocker glistened in the light of Winston Graymark's lantern as he gave it three gentle knocks. Bustling sounds were heard, and then the door was carefully opened. Oil lamps from within lit up two plump little people, a man and a woman, looking like forest elves in their nightshirts, their moss green woolen robes, and their green-and-white-striped nightcaps.

"Oh, Master Win, we'd quite given you up!" exclaimed the little woman.

"That we had!" said the little man, bobbing his head. "Else we wouldn't be in our nightshirts and caps."

"You have no need to apologize, Mr. and Mrs. Cubby. It's I who must apologize for arriving here much later than I had expected," said Winston Graymark. "But as you see, in accordance with the note I sent you by Sampson, I've brought you the child. I do ask that you not let her out front of your cottage, for she should not be seen in the village."

"Oh, we'll make her comfortable, Master Win," said Mrs. Cubby. "You may be certain of that."

"I am indeed," said Winston Graymark. "As I wrote, I ask that she stay here a day or two, until Sampson comes to fetch her. And now, Mr. Cubby, if I could have the aid of your sturdy shoulder to get back into the cart, I'll be off."

"You won't stay for a cup of tea, Master Win?" asked Mrs. Cubby.

"Thank you, no, Mrs. Cubby," said Winston Graymark. "The hour is much too late, and I have kept you up long enough. Another time, and I'll be delighted to join you in a cup." Then, with Mr. Cubby's help, he was back in his cart. Mr. and Mrs. Cubby stood in the doorway waving to him until he and his cart were swallowed up by the fog.

Mrs. Cubby now turned her full attention to Jenny. "I don't

know if Master Win thought to tell you, dear, that I was his nurse-maid when he was very little. So that's the person you have come to, and now you must be shown your bed in the loft. But first wouldn't you like a cup of milk?"

Jenny nodded, too overcome to speak.

And then, suddenly, because everything was so different from what she had been imagining it would be; because instead of standing by the edge of a steep cliff or some other frightening place, she found herself standing in a cozy cottage with lace cur-tains at the windows and a fat cat asleep in the windowsill; and especially because she was standing before a small dumpling of a woman with kindly, warm, gentle gray eyes asking simply if she would like a cup of milk, Jenny burst into tears.

And felt a pair of soft arms instantly wrapped around her. "Oh, you poor child! You poor, poor, dear child!" said Mrs. Cubby.

Chapter XVIII

Grim Revelations

𝕸

For two days, Jenny felt as if she really must be asleep and dreaming. She was not allowed to wash so much as one dish or pick up a dust cloth. And as for laundry?

"Certainly not!" said Mrs. Cubby indignantly when Jenny offered to help with it. Mrs. Cubby even insisted on washing and mending Jenny's own dress, which sorely needed it, while Jenny sat wrapped in a cocoon of Mrs. Cubby's ample moss green robe.

Beyond that, all Jenny did each day was wander about in a tiny garden behind the cottage, watch the delighted Mr. Cubby at his carpentry, and pet Saucer, the big tabby cat.

But she knew the dream must end, for was she not to be fetched and taken back to Graymark House? Once again she would return to her dank cellar room, and begin again the round of facing piles of dirty dishes, dusty rooms, and mountains of dirty laundry.

Sure enough, early in the evening of Jenny's second day with Mr. and Mrs. Cubby, a cart pulled up to the doorway. It was Sampson, come to fetch Jenny. All too quickly, she was seated in the cart looking back at Mr. and Mrs. Cubby smiling and waving to her from the doorway, and rapidly vanishing into the fog that had once again rolled in. When Jenny looked back a second time, Mr. and Mrs. Cubby and their storybook cottage had disappeared entirely.

Where they had been was only darkness. To Jenny, it seemed as if they had never been there at all.

The journey back to Graymark House did little to raise her spirits. For while Sampson had greeted her with a cheerful smile, no sooner had they started out than he began to grump about the weather, and to offer the hope that they would not get knocked off the road by the careless driver of another vehicle, and might live to see morning. The ride was mercifully short, as the one going had been, but it did not end as Jenny expected it would, with the cart going directly to the stable. Instead, Sampson stopped at the front door of Graymark House.

"Climb on out, miss," said Sampson as Jenny continued to sit, waiting for him to drive on.

"H-H-Here?" asked Jenny. "But . . . but why?"

"On account o' Master Win says so," replied Sampson. "And I ain't got the foggiest . . . excusing the expression, Miss Jenny . . . as to why. Never told me neither why you was drug off middle o' the night. Ain't none o' my business, anyways. But you're to ring the doorbell to get in. And here's your carpetbag," he said after Jenny had clambered down. "Think you can manage it?"

Jenny had not been asked this question in so long, she nearly dropped the carpetbag when Sampson handed it down to her. Then he politely waited as she thumped and bumped up the steps of the portico and rang the bell before he finally drove off. Jenny was now standing alone on the fog-filled portico just as she had been on the night she arrived. This time, however, it seemed she had no sooner rung the bell than the door opened. There stood the same old man, now known to be Crimpit, exactly as had happened that first night. Was she to be asked the same questions, and looked at with the same narrowed, suspicious eyes as she had been then?

"Come in, please, miss, and follow me," was all Crimpit said, however, his face with not one shred of expression on it.

Jenny began again to feel as if she were moving in a dream as she stepped into the house. Once again she was in the high-ceilinged entry hall with the angry ocean paintings on the walls, the snarling lion's head, and the ominously coiled dragon, all guarding the ghosts that hung in the guise of portraits on the walls of the hall above. But this was not a dream. It was all real and terribly familiar. And so was the scene in the library when she was led there by Crimpit.

Seated in the red leather armchair before the embers of a log fire burning in the great stone fireplace, a man sat with one leg resting on an ottoman, the other thrown carelessly over the arm of the chair. Sitting on the floor, cross-legged, was a boy with sandy hair tumbling over his forehead. They were, of course, Winston Graymark and Jingle, who was staring at Jenny as if she were some foreign object never seen by him before. His jaw was slack, and his bright blue eyes as wide as any saucer known to man.

For a few moments, all was silence but for the crackling embers and the *ticktocking* of the tall clock in the corner of the room. And then there was heard faintly the sound of horses' hooves and carriage wheels crunching up the driveway. Winston Graymark looked up at the clock. "Right on time, I see," he said.

"Should I go speak to them, Master Win?" asked Crimpit.

"No, no," he replied. "That won't be necessary, Crimpit. They've been advised that they're to wait where they are. Just take Jenny's coat, if you would." He reached down with his hand and tousled Jingle's hair. "All right, Jingle, you may now run up and tell Madame Dupray I'm ready to see her and Violet."

Jingle wasted no time in scrambling from the floor and running from the room, giving Jenny only the quickest sideways glance as he passed by her. But Jenny, even though her coat had been taken by Crimpit, was left to stand in the middle of the room. Winston Graymark simply sat staring into the fireplace without another word. He seemed to have forgotten all about her.

At last, Jingle returned with Madame Dupray and Violet, and

Jenny could see at once that something was very wrong with Violet. Her face was frozen and drained of all color. She stared rigidly ahead without so much as a glance at Jenny. Could it be that Madame Dupray had revealed Violet's theft to Winston Graymark? That now Violet was to be confronted with her crime, and Jenny was there to be a witness to it? Oh, no, surely no one could be so cruel as to make Jenny do that!

But when Madame Dupray caught sight of Jenny, she started with surprise. Her face instantly hardened, and her lips tightened.

"Yes, as you can see, Madame Dupray," said Winston Graymark, "Jenny has been found."

"And where was she found?" asked Madame Dupray, biting off each word.

"In the stable all along," replied Winston Graymark, coolly lying. "It is my understanding she was out there visiting some new puppies, and fell asleep. She slept so long, she was afraid to show herself back in the house. Jingle, I'm sorry to say, was contributing to this escapade by delivering food to her."

"For two whole days?" asked Madame Dupray.

In reply, Winston Graymark merely shrugged and produced his twisted grin.

"Jenny, how could you do such a thing?" said Madame Dupray, who in truth could hardly say much to Jingle, Winston Graymark's personal "valley." But her eyes when she looked at Jenny were hard and glittering with anger. "How could you betray me in such a way when I stood by you and persuaded Mr. Graymark not to send you away? You put me in a very bad light, Jenny."

"Madame Dupray, there is no need to say more," said Winston Graymark. "Jenny has been very contrite, and I'm certain will never try such a thing again."

Again? But Jenny had never done what she was being accused of in the first place! Why did Winston Graymark make up such a story? What was the reason for taking her away from Graymark

House in the middle of the night, and now lying about it? Did he *want* to put Madame Dupray in a bad light? If so, he had certainly succeeded. She had been a good friend to Jenny, and had every right to feel betrayed by her, and every right to be angry.

But why was Violet there? Nothing was being said about her stealing from Winston Graymark's wine decanter, yet she looked as if she were going to faint. Did she not realize that this whole meeting had to do with Jenny, and Jenny alone? And now the meeting appeared to be over.

"Mr. Graymark," said Madame Dupray, a polite voice masking her anger, "for some reason you asked that Violet be here tonight, but that has left Mr. Graymark, Sr. alone. With your permission, Violet and I will now excuse ourselves, as your business with me has, I believe, ended."

"No, not quite ended, Madame Dupray," said Winston Graymark evenly. With great deliberation, he lifted one leg down from the arm of his chair, the other from the ottoman. "You see, Violet has made a confession to me."

Madame Dupray drew back, her eyes widened in shock. "Oh, Mr. Graymark!" she cried, wringing her hands. "Oh, it was good of Violet to have told you what she did, but it is I who should have done so. I did not because I knew how much she needed this position and felt if you were told, she would be instantly dismissed. Now I know I should have put your welfare ahead of hers. But I do apologize with deepest regret. And if you keep her on, all I can say is that I give you my solemn word it will never, never happen again."

"I should hope it doesn't," said Winston Graymark, grimacing. "I shouldn't like to think that every time I had a drink from this decanter, I'd be helping myself to a glass of poison."

Madame Dupray gasped. "Poison!"

Winston Graymark shrugged. "Yes, Madame Dupray. It seems that what Jenny saw in the library was *not* Violet helping herself to a drink from my decanter, but administering poison to it."

"Are you quite certain about this, Mr. Graymark?" asked Madame Dupray.

"Oh, yes!" he replied. "I had my chemist check it out. Fortunately, it wasn't advisable for me to drop dead instantly, it seems, so the poison was of the variety that needed to be taken over a number of days, perhaps even weeks. Because I felt so ill, I drank no wine three nights ago, and have had none since, thanks to Violet's warning."

Madame Dupray turned sharply to face Violet. "Is what Mr. Graymark said true? If so, what is the meaning of it, Violet? What could you possibly hope to gain by this terrible act? Did you believe that with Mr. Graymark gone, you might be able to stay on here? Oh, that is despicable!"

But before the nearly paralyzed Violet could get her wits together to speak, Winston Graymark broke in. "Madame Dupray, before you continue, you had better know that Violet has informed me what she did was at your orders."

Madame Dupray drew herself up, her jaws clenched. "If that is what Violet has told you, then she is lying," she snapped. "What possible reason could I have for ordering her to do such a villainous act?"

"Why, every reason in the world," replied Winston Graymark smoothly. "I believe that you and my . . . my *trusted* employee, who is also your great, good friend, Obadiah Slorkin, conspired to have my father sign a will one day a short time ago, believing him to be senile as well as frail and with poor eyesight. It was a will leaving all of the Graymark fortune to the two of you if I should not be living at the time of my father's death. You, of course, were planning to insure that I was not living."

"What proof do you have of this nonsense, Mr. Graymark?" Madame Dupray inquired icily.

"Proof enough," he replied.

"I doubt it," said Madame Dupray. "But you are grossly insulting me, and as I do not care to continue standing here and be so maligned, I shall take my leave."

"Oh, not so quickly," said Winston Graymark. "There is still the matter of Jenny to be explained."

"I believe that has already been explained. It is not to my satisfaction, but it has, at least, been explained. Please come with me, Violet." Madame Dupray turned on her heel and started from the room.

"No, not entirely explained, Madame Dupray," said Winston Graymark, putting his chin on his hands, watching as she hesitated and turned back. "There is still the little matter of your ordering Violet to contrive to get Jenny out to the cliff and then send her over it to kingdom come."

"Beyond the fact that Violet is lying yet again," said Madame Dupray, her eyes flashing, "why should I want any such thing to happen to Jenny? Have you forgotten, sir, that it was I who persuaded you to allow her to stay here rather than have her shipped back to China to who knows what fate?"

"No, I have not," replied Winston Graymark. "But as her 'fate,' as you put it, was not assured if she were sent away, and she might grow up to learn things you had rather she never learn, I believe you wanted her kept here so you could see that she did not live long enough for that to happen."

"Mr. Graymark, you appear to be very good at guessing," said Madame Dupray. "Perhaps you can guess any reason I might have to care what happens to this Jenny Bekins other than the kindness of my heart in persuading you to keep her here?"

Winston Graymark gave a weary sigh. "Oh, Madame Dupray, I have no need to guess anything. All the answers are right here." With that, he reached down beside him and drew out a packet of letters tied in a red ribbon, holding them up for her to see.

At the sight of the letters, Madame Dupray staggered, her

long, pale fingers clutching her throat. Her face turned a ghastly white. "Who . . . who gave you those?" she whispered hoarsely.

"I did! I did!" Violet cried out. Then she threw her face into her hands, sobbing.

"You little fool!" Madame Dupray hissed. "But what gave you the right to read *my* letters, Mr. Graymark?" She turned to him furiously.

"Why, I suppose whatever it was that gave you the right to steal a letter addressed to my father," he returned without so much as blinking. "It is, of course, the letter written by Jenny's mother telling of her marriage to my brother, and of Jenny's birth."

"What difference would the letter have made?" asked Madame Dupray. "You said you would not believe the letter even if you had seen it."

"Oh, easy enough to say when I'd never seen it, wouldn't you agree?" said Winston Graymark. "In any event, that was certainly not a judgment for *you* to make, Madame Dupray. But now we come to the other letters, the ones written to you all these years by one who was your friend when you were dance hall girls together, Jenny's mother. So though I knew nothing of it, you knew of her marriage to my brother, and of Jenny's birth.

"You knew that Jenny was being sent here, and of the letter that was sent announcing her arrival, and in truth, explaining her very existence. Desperate not to have this known, you watched and waited for that letter to arrive, and when it did, you purloined it. In your further desperation, you even went so far as to have Violet ransack Jenny's trunk and her whole room, lest there be some tiny evidence pointing to her being another living heir to the Graymark fortune. So, yes, I can indeed guess why you would care what happens to Jenny, Madame Maisie Dupray!"

"*Maisie* Dupray?" said Madame Dupray archly, a sudden, sly flicker in her eyes. "But that is my sister, for whom I have little use. If you had noted the envelopes, you would see that they were sent to her at her address in the city. *I,* as you well know, am *Hermione* Dupray. So you see, Mr. Graymark, you are quite wrong about everything."

"Come, come, Madame Dupray!" said Winston Graymark. "We both know Maisie Dupray and Hermione Dupray are one and the same person. I've recently pried out of Obadiah Slorkin the admission that the 'sister' was an invention to keep his close friendship with you from my attention. He knew that the Maisie Dupray of his acquaintance was, while an excellent actress, no more from a noble French family fallen on hard times than I was, and would not have been the kind of person I would have wished to look after my father."

"Obadiah!" Madame Dupray spat out. "And what will you say to him of all this?"

"All this . . . and more," said Winston Graymark. "For, of course, as you must know, while he left the poisoning up to you, he was also trying to insure my demise by having my cart tampered with, in case the poisoning effort failed. There are many loyal employees at Graymark Shipping, and they were able to discover that the prankster I believed was the culprit was someone enlisted by no other than Obadiah Slorkin! Further, good friends that you are, I'm sure you know he has also been tampering with the Graymark Shipping till ever since my father left, something I recently uncovered. Oh, yes, Madame Dupray, he will be dealt with, you may be sure of that.

"But as to that sister of yours, you do in very truth have a sister, and she is right here in this room. She is Violet Dupray, whom you tried, but most fortunately failed, to turn into someone as evil as you!"

Madame Dupray again faced the quietly sobbing Violet. "You fool! You little idiot! I trusted you with the secrets of my trunk, even with the very key to it, and look what you have done with that trust. You have ruined your chances for a life of comfort and ease, which I would have seen to it that you had. Well, now you can stay in a filthy cellar for the rest of your life, or marry some village idiot like the one Lilly has found for herself."

"Stay in a filthy cellar for the rest of your life!" Almost the same words Jenny had heard through the wall on her first night in the cellar. But now she knew they had not been spoken out of concern for her. No, they were a warning to *Violet!*

Now Violet raised her tear-stained face, revealing a mixture of anger and misery. "I don't care, Maisie. I would rather have that life than live one out as a *murderer!* You have been in a jealous rage all these years because you always believed you had lost Cameron Graymark to Jenny's mother, and lost his fortune along with him. And you would even use your own sister to gain your wicked ends!"

"Well, stay here, then, in your cellar room," snarled Madame Dupray. "You have lost your last chance of ever leaving it!"

"I wouldn't say that, Madame Dupray," Winston Graymark broke in quickly. "Nor need you have fears on any other score. Although Violet enjoys Lilly's cheerful company and has felt friendly toward her, she in no way wishes to follow in Lilly's footsteps. And I intend to see that she does not have to. But I can absolutely assure you that tonight will be the last night she ever spends in a cellar room!"

"It's no longer anything to me," said Madame Dupray coldly. "But it is clear that *I* can no longer remain here, Mr. Graymark. I shall pack tonight, and make arrangements to leave tomorrow."

"On the contrary," said Winston Graymark, "you will be leaving tonight. Crimpit, if you will now summon the gentlemen who have been waiting patiently in the driveway, they will escort Madame Dupray out. At my request, Violet has packed a small bag for you, Madame Dupray; it is at the front door. Everything else you have here will be sent to whatever place you advise Crimpit. But before you go, you might like to know that I hold the will in hand that you and Slorkin so artfully arranged, and here is what I intend to do with it."

Slowly and deliberately, Winston Graymark crushed the sheets of paper into a ball and threw them on the burning embers in the fireplace.

"I'm sure, of course, that Obadiah has a copy as well," he said, "as I doubt either one of you trusts the other to own the only one. But for what it's worth, he may as well treat his copy to the same fate. And it might interest the two of you to know that my 'senile, frail' father must have been suspicious of what he was signing, for he wrote another will in his own hand, making no mention of either of you, and it now reposes in that wall safe, courtesy of Crimpit. So the two of you might well have ended up with blood on your hands, and not one thing to show for it.

"Dear me," he added with a clearly false look of dismay. "Now it comes to me, you never needed to steal the letter, either. You see, I've had people on the West Coast doing some detective work for me. At long last, I finally received a letter today that happily fell into my own hands and not yours, Madame Dupray. It seems that they have found the records attesting to the fact that a child was born to Cameron and Kitty Graymark. What happened after that, of course, you and I both know from the letter.

"Oh, and before you go, there is still something else that might interest you. Jenny has not been in the stable. You see, when I learned of the plan you had to kidnap her and have everyone believe she had run away, never to be heard from again—after Violet was unable to do what you so cruelly asked of her—I simply arranged to beat you at your game, and kidnapped Jenny myself. She's been safely kept these past days." Winston Graymark threw out his hands with a rueful grin. "I just thought you might enjoy knowing this. Now, Madame Dupray, I must bid you good evening!"

That no one left behind could see the look on her face as she attempted to sweep from the room with disdain was probably all for the best.

Chapter XIX

A Joyful Welcome

🜚

After Madame Dupray had left, only the crackling embers in the fireplace, the *ticktocking* of the clock, and the sound of Violet softly sobbing into her handkerchief broke the silence in the room. Jingle sat fidgeting uncomfortably, staring down at the carpet as if something interesting were crawling across it. Jenny remained standing in the middle of the room, staring at the tall clock for want of anything else to stare at. Winston Graymark, for his part, sat studying Jenny with a bemused expression on his face.

Soon the front door was heard to close, and Crimpit came shuffling back into the library. "Is there anything more you would like of me, Master Win?" he asked.

"Has everything been taken care of out there?" Winston Graymark raised a questioning eyebrow.

"She's gone, Master Win," replied Crimpit.

"Thank you for your help, Crimpit," Winston Graymark said. "I think that will be all for tonight."

"Good night, then, Master Win," Crimpit said, and shuffled from the room.

"Jenny?" Winston Graymark said gently.

"Y-Y-Yes, Mr. Graymark," replied Jenny.

Winston Graymark shook his head. "Didn't you hear anything that went on here tonight, Jenny?" he asked. "I'm afraid you're going to have to get used to calling me something else now. I would suggest that it might be 'Uncle Win.' Do you think you can manage that?"

Jenny remained silent for a few moments. And then for a few moments longer. All that had happened was just too much for her. To suddenly learn that she was Jenny Graymark after all. To be told that this man whom she had so feared and, yes, so disliked, she was now to call "Uncle Win." Oh, she would not do it. She could not! And, yet, despite herself, she slowly nodded.

"I don't blame you for having to think about that, Jenny," Winston Graymark said with a rueful smile. "I know I've treated you abominably, and I'm very sorry for it. I won't try to excuse it, but perhaps I did have some justification for it, which I hope you will come to understand and can then forgive me a little. I'm sorry, too, about scaring you half to death by dragging you off in the middle of the night. But I knew you'd be happy with Mr. and Mrs. Cubby. And I was really afraid to tell you all I knew until Madame Dupray had been confronted." He paused to grimace. "That wasn't a very pleasant conversation with her, was it?"

Eyes fastened on the toes of her shoes, Jenny shook her head.

"Well," said Winston Graymark, "now it's time for us to do something that's *very* pleasant. I think we ought to go up right away and let my father know that he has a granddaughter. Would you like that, Jenny?"

"Oh, yes!" said Jenny at once, for there was surely no need to hesitate over *this* question.

"Splendid!" said Winston Graymark. "Violet, you won't be needed any further for my father tonight. But you don't have to spend another night in the cellar if you don't wish it. We can certainly find you a room upstairs, where you'll now be staying."

"Thank you, Mr. Graymark," Violet replied, looking at him with eyes still brimming with tears. "But you have a great deal to talk about now, and it *is* growing late."

"Perhaps you're right," he said. "We'll take care of your room tomorrow morning. And I might add that *we* have a great deal to talk about as well, Violet."

Violet hesitated. "With . . . with your permission, Mr. Graymark, may I say something to Jenny before I go?"

"Of course!" he said quickly.

"Jenny," Violet said, turning to her, "when I came to you the other night and confessed that I had not been as kind to you as I might, I never did explain why that was. I'd like to do that now. But to begin with, I must tell you that my sister took care of me from the time our parents died, and I always looked up to her, even though, for some reason, I did not always share her ideas. I felt for a time I had no choice but to go along with her terrible plans, no matter what they might be. But when she asked me to be friendly toward you, to win your trust so I could more easily help her carry out the wicked deed she wanted of me, I tried, but could not do it. For how could I be friends with someone when I knew the horrible fate in store for her? In the end, I knew it all to be impossible, and that's why I finally went to Mr. Graymark. I only hope you can understand all this, Jenny. And, again, I ask your forgiveness."

"And I give it to you again, Violet," said Jenny, tears flooding her own eyes.

"Thank you, Jenny. And thank you once more, Mr. Graymark," said Violet. And though her cheeks were still wet with tears, she managed to give them both a grateful smile as she departed the room.

Winston Graymark then reached down to pat Jingle on the head. "Well, I guess you can retire to your quarters as well, imp."

"Oh, Mr. . . . Mr. . . . " Jenny stopped in confusion. "I . . . I mean Uncle . . . Uncle Win, can't Jingle come with us, too?" she asked. For in truth she was still a little frightened of this new uncle, and afraid of how she should behave alone with him.

"Oh, why not?" he said. "Jingle's becoming as much a part of the family as anyone else. And I've been getting the feeling that you two are growing thick as thieves. All right, then, you can come with us, imp!"

Finally thawing from his frozen condition, Jingle grinned and jumped up from the floor.

Jenny was in a daze as she climbed the stairs, this time not as Jenny Bekins but as Jenny Graymark. And there she was, walking down the gallery with the eyes of the portraits fixed upon her. What were they thinking now, now that she was no longer a servant but actually belonged at Graymark House?

"These are your ancestors, Jenny," Winston Graymark said. "The old horrors! That's your great-aunt Mehitabel, and here is your great-uncle Josiah. These are old Cousins Drusilla and Horace. I hated them when I was your age, and often thought when I grew up I'd take them all down. Now I've just grown used to them."

"What's that bare spot, Mr. Winston?" Jingle asked. "You've never said."

"You've never asked, Jingle," he replied. "But that was a portrait of . . . of . . . ," he faltered. "of my brother, Cam, Jenny's father, and me when we were boys. We were actually smiling, too. I think the rest of them disapproved. When I stopped hearing from him, I took it down. It made me sad to see it. But perhaps I might just put it back up again. Then you can see a portrait of your papa when he was your age, Jenny."

Jenny's papa, Cameron Graymark! Had she ever thought to hear that at Graymark House? Jenny was too overcome to speak.

But now they were approaching old Mr. Graymark's room, and her heart had begun to race. How would he feel about his new granddaughter? Her golden curls were gone. She was wearing a dress that, while washed and mended by Mrs. Cubby, had grown worn and shabby from doing dirty dishes and dusty rooms and dirty laundry. Had old Mr. Graymark cared about that when she read to him, brought him the puppy, and held the ink pot for him as he wrote? No, but that was when she was only the little servant girl. Would he—could he feel the same knowing that this was Jenny Graymark, his granddaughter?

Yet, oh how little Jenny need have worried about it! For when Winston Graymark brought her into the room and told his father who Jenny really was, the look on old Mr. Graymark's face, the tears streaming down his cheeks, were all she needed to know how she was welcomed as his granddaughter. Not to mention the hugging and the kisses on her own cheeks that her newfound grandfather could not seem to get enough of.

The first order of business after that joyful moment was, of course, for Winston Graymark to tell his father how Jenny had first come to Graymark House, and of all that had happened since, especially the events that had just transpired in the library.

"Villainous! Villainous!" old Mr. Graymark exclaimed over and over. And then finally he said, "So I was right! Those papers Slorkin shoved under my nose to sign *were* a will with his name and that of Madame Dupray on it. I should have objected to signing anything even though Slorkin told me they were all papers pertaining to Graymark Shipping, of which I'm still nominal head. But my eyes are bad, and it was all done so quickly."

"Don't blame yourself, Father," said Winston Graymark. "You were clever enough to think of writing that new will. Oh, yes, I know about that. When Violet brought me the letters and the will done by Slorkin, I went to the safe just to check on the old one, which you've never kept a secret from me, and there I found your handwritten one, dated *after* Slorkin's, together with your note to Crimpit, charging him to tell me of the will should anything happen to you. It didn't take much to put all the pieces of the puzzle together. But what I can't understand is why you never told me of your suspicions?"

"Well," replied old Mr. Graymark with a shrug, "assuming I

could get you to believe me, I felt the first thing you'd do was confront Slorkin and Madame Dupray. And what proof would you have had, the word of an old man whose brain, it could easily be argued, was impaired from a stroke? All I might have brought myself was the wrath of Madame Dupray and a closer watch of my every move."

"I only wish you could have told me your feelings about her," said Winston Graymark.

"Would you have believed me?" asked old Mr. Graymark. "You and I haven't had the closest relationship these past years, and you seemed to have such a high regard for Madame Dupray's every opinion of the state of my health."

"I did, and I can't forgive myself for putting so much trust in her," said Winston Graymark. "And, of course, you're right. Had you persuaded me of your suspicions, I might have rushed right out to confront her and Slorkin, probably with the results you suggest. It's a grim thought. But now let's leave that behind and move on to something happier, a letter I'm ready to read to you."

And so Jenny, perched on the side of the four-poster bed with her friend Jingle, now heard for the very first time the letter written by her mama to her grandfather.

She, along with her grandfather, learned how Cameron Graymark had fallen in love with Kitty O'Reilly, a hostess in a dance hall. Angered and distraught because his father was so opposed to her—his father believing that she cared more for the Graymark fortune than she did him, and claiming that he would disinherit Cameron if he ever married her—*did* marry her, and took her with him to the West Coast. In time, Jenny was born to them.

All the while, Cameron Graymark continued writing his brother, but never told him of the marriage or of the birth of his child. They had been living on very little, when the opportunity came for him to go to China, hopefully to make his fortune. Intending to tell his brother of his marriage and his child when they arrived there, he was cruelly taken from his young wife and baby.

Knowing how much his father was opposed to her, she never could bring herself to write of their marriage, of the child, or even of his death, for which she could only believe she would be blamed. She met and married Felix Bekins, and lost him as well. When she knew her own end to be near, she finally wrote the letter to Jenny's grandfather, hoping he could forgive her and his son enough to accept Jenny as the granddaughter she really was.

By the time Winston Graymark had finished reading the sad letter, tears flowed from the eyes of old Mr. Graymark. "What a fool I was!" he groaned. "What an arrogant, stupid fool! In my heart I knew Kitty O'Reilly really loved Cam, and proved it by marrying him even though she believed I would disinherit him and there would be no Graymark fortune. I really never had any intention of doing that, but neither she nor Cam had any way of knowing it. I suppose I didn't like the idea of her being a dance hall girl, proud idiot that I was. And she was such a sweet, pretty little thing. It was no wonder Cam loved her!"

"Or she him," said Winston Graymark. "Jenny, your father was as nice as he could be. Hotheaded, though, which was why he ran off the way he did, but a really handsome devil, tall and straight and good looking. It's no surprise he was your and Mother's favorite, Father."

At this, old Mr. Graymark sat up stiffly in his chair. His faded eyes suddenly flashed angrily. "Is that what you think, Win? If you do, you are dead wrong."

"And you really have never been sorry that it was Cam who was lost, and not I?" Winston Graymark said softly. "It's what I always believed, the way you started going downhill, even before the stroke, from the time we finally realized Cam was never coming back."

"Well, you always believed wrong, Win," old Mr. Graymark said, shaking his head. "What makes you think I wouldn't have gone just as 'downhill,' as you put it, if you'd been the one never to return?"

Winston Graymark shrugged. "I don't know. My being the crippled one, I suppose."

"As if that ever made any difference," said old Mr. Graymark. "You were a dear little boy, Win, and a brave one. Sometimes too brave and daring. You scared your mother half to death sometimes, but you were greatly loved. You and Cam both were . . . equally. I just don't understand why it has taken so long for this to come out. But could it be what's driven you to start doing all those angry ocean paintings?"

"I really don't have the wildest idea," said Winston Graymark with a rueful grin.

"Well, I think you had better stop, anyway, Winston, and try your hand at something more cheerful. You've done enough of those others," said old Mr. Graymark sternly.

"Yes, Papa," said Winston Graymark meekly.

At which point, old Mr. Graymark began to chuckle, and his son threw his head back, laughing.

"But I'll tell you what," he said. "I'll promise to try painting some pleasant, sunny days at the shore instead of what I've been doing, if you'll try getting up and about. I realize now it's Madame Dupray who's made a full-fledged depressed invalid out of you. Dr. Penwick says you're physically fine, and only need your spirits lifted. So we *don't* have Cam back, but we have his child . . . your granddaughter. That ought to be enough to get you down into the library again, where your leather chair is waiting for you. I'll try, if you will. Is that a fair exchange?"

"Fair enough!" said old Mr. Graymark. "But now, tell me, Win, you really wouldn't have sent this child back to China, would you?"

"Probably not," replied Winston Graymark. "But I must confess that one thing Madame Dupray did was make it easy for me to back down. I have to be grateful to her for that. But I was pretty ugly about it, though, wasn't I, Jenny?"

Jenny, suddenly finding her knees very interesting to look at, nodded.

"She's quite right to agree with that, Father," said Winston Graymark. "But please bear in mind that I would have given my soul to have Cam walking through the door that night. Instead, here came a young girl claiming to be his daughter, and at that the daughter of someone I was quite certain was the cause of his running off in the first place. I guess I was really angry and bitter about it.

"But, Jenny, I hope you still have that pretty dress you wore the night you arrived, so you can wear it to show your grandfather. And luckily hair does manage to grow out, so you'll have your long curls back in no time."

Jenny gave Jingle a sideways look. "I don't want them back," she said in a stiff little voice.

Her uncle Win's eyebrows rose. "Oh, I see," he said. "So that's how it is." He looked at the suddenly rigid Jingle, back to the now equally rigid Jenny, and apparently then decided to say no more about the subject. "At any rate, Father," he continued, "I felt I might be on uncertain turf when Jenny said she was from China. Do you remember how fascinated Cam always was with the rug at the foot of the stairs? I remember he used to sit there right in the middle of that dragon when he was very little, and announce that someday he was going to China to catch one and bring it home. Do you remember that, Father?"

"I do indeed!" he said.

As soon as Jenny heard this, she slipped quickly off the bed. Dipping her hand into her dress pocket, she drew out her little round silver box and held it out to Winston Graymark. "Here," she said, "would you like to see this, U-U-Uncle Win?"

Smiling encouragingly as Jenny struggled with the still unfamiliar name, he took the box from her. "Is this the little silver object I saw you pull out from under your cot mattress the other night?" he asked. "It must be something very precious that you had to take it with you."

"It is," said Jenny. "Mama said my real papa gave it to her."

"And it has a dragon on it, doesn't it?" Winston Graymark said. "So it looks as if our Cam finally did go to China and catch one, doesn't it, Father? And here it is back home! May I open your box, Jenny?"

"Oh, yes," she said. "And that's a bit of my baby hair in it."

"I thought it might be," Winston Graymark said. "But what's this?" He pulled gently on a bit of silk ribbon inside the cover of the box. It was so tiny and artfully blended into the pattern of the silk lining that Jenny had never even seen it. Nor, it seemed, had anyone else, for when Winston Graymark pulled on it, the entire lining of the cover, wrapped over a piece of round cardboard, lifted right out. Under it was a small piece of very thin, folded paper.

"Did you know about this?" he asked Jenny. When she shook her head, he said, "May I?" When she then nodded to him, he unfolded the paper and read the words written on it.

"'To my darling wife, Kitty, upon the birth of our baby, Guinevere.' It's in Cam's handwriting. Here, Father, look."

Old Mr. Graymark took the bit of paper, and when he saw the familiar handwriting on it, his eyes welled with tears again.

"B-B-But," stammered Jenny, "my name is not Guinevere." Suddenly she saw all this newly gained happiness crumbling into hopelessly tiny pieces.

Winston Graymark burst into laughter. "Of course it is! Guinevere was your grandmother's name, and Jenny is the short name for Guinevere. But, oh, Jenny, Jenny, would that you'd known of this and shown it to me. What a world of misery it would have saved. I only hope you can forgive your uncle Win for all he has done. Can you?"

"Oh, yes!" cried Jenny, fast as any heartbeat. For having heard all the explanations, how could she not forgive him? And she was now even beginning to understand why Jingle was so devoted to him.

For a while, conversation ended as old Mr. Graymark read the precious note over and over again. But at last he handed it back to his son to have it placed carefully back in the silver box, and then looked at Jenny with a sudden twinkle in his eyes. "Now when, my darling granddaughter, are you and Jingle going to bring that puppy back to see me?"

Upon hearing this, Winston Graymark's head snapped up. "What's this about bringing a puppy *back?* Were you two monkeys here with one before?" Suddenly a strange look crossed his face. His eyebrows rose, and his eyes widened. "I don't know why I never stopped to wonder about it, but was that also the time you wrote that new will, Father?"

"It was," replied old Mr. Graymark, smiling at his grand-daughter. "And Jenny helped by going to fetch the proper tools for it from the library. The children, of course, had no idea what I was up to, and I swore them to secrecy."

"My, but you are a sly trio!" said Winston Graymark with a broad grin. "But how did you manage it under the eagle eyes of Madame Dupray? You know, Father, that woman never allowed Jenny in this room unless she or Violet was present. She said some-thing to me about it disturbing you. Now I know the real reason. She didn't want Jenny talking to you about her past life lest you actually believed her. So how *did* you two get a puppy in here?"

"Oh, we ain't done nothing wrong, Mr. Winston," Jingle burst forth as Jenny sat twisting her fingers uncomfortably. "It was when Violet—"

But Jenny stopped him. "Jingle, we mustn't say anything about—"

"It's quite all right, Jenny," Winston Graymark said quickly. "I think I know how it happened, and you don't have to worry about Violet's part in this. She's already confessed to skipping out to see Lilly, and the subject is now closed.

"But, Jingle, about that 'ain't done nothing wrong.' Would you like to repeat that in a manner that doesn't make my ears hurt? I've been letting you off lightly of late. It wasn't awfully important when it was just a matter of your being my valet, or of working in the stable, and it's going to be a while before I drag you kicking and screaming into a position at Graymark Shipping. But right now you're spending a lot of time with your friend, who happens to be my niece. So, do you mind, Jingle?"

"Sampson talks same as I do," said Jingle, his jaw set stubbornly. "How come you never say nothing 'bout that?"

"Because Sampson's an old man who's been here since the year one, so I can't worry about that. But, please, no more arguing, imp. Let's have it again."

"I ain't . . . ," Jingle began, and then thought better of it. He sighed deeply. "We did . . . did . . . did not do noth–noth . . . anything wrong," he said, his face flushed with the effort.

"Splendid!" said Winston Graymark. "Now do it again."

"We did not do anything wrong," Jingle said, and then, realizing what he had accomplished, gave a proud grin.

"Now I have an idea," said Winston Graymark. "Why don't you two run down to the stable and bring back said puppy right now? Of course, it *is* getting pretty late. Would you be too tired for this, Father?"

"Not at all!" replied Mr. Graymark wholeheartedly.

"I've dismissed Violet for the evening, Father," Winston Graymark said. "While those two are gone, I can help you prepare for the night. And there are just one or two things we might find to start talking about. I'd like your ideas on how we can bring some life back to this house, the way it was when Cam and I were growing up here. Do you remember the parties you and Mother used to have for us? And I think we need to think about fixing up that little cottage on the grounds for the Crimpits to retire to. Perhaps we can get Mr. and Mrs. Cubby back for a while until we get everything sorted out. . . ."

Old Mr. Graymark threw up his hands, laughing. "Enough, Win. I can already see that my resting days are over."

"Well, you two can get going," Winston Graymark said, waving Jenny and Jingle off. "But before you leave, I think that my father would agree with me that you shouldn't spend another night in the cellar, Jenny. I believe you know all the rooms up here. Which one do you think you'd like for your own?"

Jenny did not need a single moment to think about this. "I want the room across from Grandfather," she said.

"But that's the smallest room up here," said Winston Graymark. "It used to be my mother's sewing room and it's not much bigger than a large closet. Don't you want to choose another one?"

"No, Uncle Win," said Jenny, her jaw set stubbornly. "That's the one I want."

Winston Graymark threw his hands up helplessly. "All right, then. When you return with the puppy, Jingle, you can bring Jenny's carpetbag with you. We'll get her other things from the cellar in the morning. Now you two run along. And, Jingle, don't go pushing out the door ahead of Jenny. What about those manners I've been trying to teach you?"

With another sigh, Jingle stepped aside for Jenny.

As they walked down the gallery, Jenny looked up at the portraits and suddenly found herself thinking that there were her great-aunt Mehitabel and her great-uncle Josiah. No, they were her uncle Win's and her papa's great-aunt Mehitabel and great-uncle Josiah. To Jenny, they would be her great-great, or was it—? Oh, it was all confusing. But what delightful confusion! Why was Jingle so glum, especially considering the mission they were on, actually going to fetch a puppy without having to be afraid of anything or anyone?

"Whatever is wrong, Jingle?" she asked.

"Oh, all fine for you," said Jingle gloomily. "No more cellar room. No more dishes. No more dusting. No more laundry. What I got now all on 'count of you is talking proper and creeping manners. I might just run away and go to sea. I wish I was a . . . a horse! *They* don't got . . . I mean, they don't have to talk proper, and think 'bout dumb manners."

"Don't be silly," said Jenny. "Horses have lots of other things they get ordered to do. And I think you should be glad Uncle Win cares about you and cares what happens to you. But you might as well know, if you don't always talk properly and have manners around *me*, I'll never say one word about it. So there!"

Jingle finally managed a grin, although it vanished almost as soon as it appeared. "What 'bout *them?*" he said, jerking a thumb up at the portraits.

"You're being silly again. They're only painted pictures," said Jenny. "They can't say anything. Remember when you told me that?"

"Not what I meant," said Jingle. "I meant how you believed you was . . . were being spooked by them. I don't want them coming round spooking me if I don't do something right."

"Oh, they won't," said Jenny. "Besides, I don't believe all that anymore about spooking or ghosts or anything. They . . . they're my . . . my relations. Everything is . . . everything is . . . different now. . . ."

Was it? Jenny's voice trailed off uncertainly as she looked up at the portraits and saw those same fixed eyes staring at her. Then suddenly she saw Great-Great-Uncle Josiah wink at her, and the corners of Great-Great-Aunt Mehitabel's mouth turn up in what would certainly have to be called a smile. Jenny blinked, blinked again, and their faces turned as stiff and solemn as ever. But she had seen the wink and the smile. She *had!* Still, did it matter as long as she believed that she had? And she *did* believe it!

"Are you certain 'bout that?" asked Jingle. "I mean 'bout how it's all different now?"

Jenny looked up and exchanged knowing looks with her ancestors. "Oh, yes!" she said happily. "I'm quite, *quite* certain!"